To every girl who has ever been called the f-word.
You're beautiful. Believe it.

While I stumble on the floor of your room
Flushed when you look at me...
Never you mind
When I love you imperfectly
Darling you will find
My heart has perfect memory.

- JAY E. TRIA, Songs of Our Breakup

IF·THE·DRESS FITS

one

"One order of chicken nuggets, a cheeseburger, large fries and Coke please," I chirped into the speaker box of the drive-thru before leaning back in my seat.

After a moment's hesitation, I slid my window down again.

"And…could you please add a caramel sundae? Thanks."

From my place in the back seats, I could hear our driver chuckling while my mother shook her head with fake solemnity. I scowled and kicked the back of their seats as the attendant repeated my order and instructed our car to drive to the next window.

"They really starved you on that budget flight, huh?" Our driver, Benjo, teased as I rolled my eyes and paid for my drive-thru meal.

"Ha-ha, Kuya," I said, hoping he could see me in the mirror rolling my eyes at him. "I haven't eaten since yesterday."

"Yesterday has only been yesterday for about an hour, Martha," My mother pointed out, as Benjo chortled and passed the food from the restaurant window to me. I scowled at him through his rear view mirror. Then our car sped off, as fast as cars could in Manila, towards the general direction of home.

"Seoul is one hour ahead of Manila, so…" I pointed out. There was a moment of silence while I started on the fries. Perfection.

I may not know a lot of things, but I do know that there is no hunger pang in the world that cannot be solved by salty, greasy french fries from the nearest fast food chain.

The truth was, I hadn't eaten since six pm the night before because I was in transit. I barely had time to buy food in Incheon, so a midnight drive-thru before going home was essential. Mom knew that, of course, but she lived to tease.

I spent the last week in South Korea attending an ASEAN integration conference for accountants. Not my first time to fly to Seoul, but it was my first time to see the city in the fall. It was so pretty, with all the orange autumn leaves crunching at your feet and the cool breeze accompanying you on your long walks. I missed the weather already.

The only thing Manila and Seoul seemed to share weather-wise was the occasional rain, and even then Manila managed to make rain awful by magically conjuring freak traffic along the major roads during every downpour. Tonight was no exception.

"You should go on a diet while it's still easy for you, dear," My mother said with a tiny sigh. "Look at me and your father. We survive on salads now because we didn't watch our eating habits when we were young."

I wasn't really in the mood to debate my eating choices past midnight, so I simply shrugged and said, "You only live once, Mom."

"Aw, honey, nobody says YOLO anymore," my Mom laughed before reaching over to grab a fry from my box.

I knew she had a point, though. Most girls my age in this country were beautiful, with slim, petite bodies and on the verge of the next stage of their life—getting married, having boyfriends, getting engaged, getting their dream jobs and getting likes for their 'side-hustles' and #fitnessgoals.

I also knew that I was nothing like the girls my age. I was a 200-pound blip in that statistic, still single and spending my money on costumes for my dog and Korean street food.

My relationship with food was long, simple, and absolutely delicious. My relationship with my weight was a little more complicated. I carried it around, and I was good at making it look effortless. It wasn't something I loved or hated, it was just a fact that I accepted. I know I'm supposed to "love my size," and I did. But forgive me for not being totally happy with it 24/7.

I felt like I was still waiting for my life to begin, but my weight had nothing to do with that.

* * *

It was nearly two in the morning when we pulled into the driveway, but finally, we were home.

"Ate Mar-thaaaa!" My little sister Maggie greeted, practically running across the foyer from the kitchen as I entered the house sans my shoes, as was our custom. Mom says it's to keep the hardwood floors clean.

Running up behind Maggie with his tail wagging wildly was Bibi, the sweet, clumsy little Shih tzu I bought with my second salary. My first pay, as tradition, was used to buy dinner for my family, and Bibi was my first big Life Purchase. Getting a dog with my own money was a promise I made to myself as a child, and taking care of Bibi helped me feel just a little less lonely.

I still remember seeing baby Bibi in the pet shop in Cartimar, all alone and shivering in a small corner of a cage. Now he craved constant affection and always got himself into little bumps and accidents as a result of his own enthusiasm.

Between Maggie and Bibi, Bibi reached me first (not before he slipped on the floor), rose up to his hind legs and offered me his paws and his big brown eyes. He looked so excited, I picked him up first, giggling when he kept trying to use my breasts as paw-holds and was so excited he couldn't stay still. The plastic cone around his head smacked me in the face a couple of times as he adjusted himself.

"Bibi!" I cooed, scratching him near his tail as we cuddled. He was forever getting into little scrapes and slips, and it wasn't uncommon for me to see him with a plastic cone on. This was our usual routine, and if I didn't know any better, I would say that he probably missed me.

"Oh sure, we don't see each other for a week, and you say hi to Bibi first," Maggie said, rolling her eyes and placing a hand on her hip as she chewed on a granola bar for a midnight snack. She's been spending most of her time in the gym lately to slim down, and I had to say, it was working. Mags had already dropped a dress size before I left for Seoul, and after not seeing her for a week, I could see the results. "Did you buy me presents from Korea? Clothes, perhaps?"

I snorted as I put Bibi down.

"They don't believe in anything bigger than size medium in Seoul, unfortunately. I did get you makeup though," I explained.

Bibi lingered by my legs, cautiously sniffing at the cute new socks I picked up in Hongdae while Mags and I walked to the living room, where Benjo had already deposited my luggage. Maggie flopped onto the couch while I slowly eased myself on it so it didn't break (it's happened before).

"Where's Dad?" I asked. Ellen, our housemaid, served us a hefty plate of shiny banana-cues (her snack staple). The sweet plantains, fried in brown sugar and skewered on barbecue sticks, made my mouth water. I knew I just had a large meal on the way home, but my willpower was no match for those shiny caramel bits.

Food has always been a part of my life. I ate when I was happy, when I was sad, when I was bored and sometimes when I was sleepy. It's part of my growing up, and most of my memories are associated and celebrated with it. I didn't hate that I liked to eat. In fact I liked that about myself.

What I hated were the little 'issues' that came with my size. Strapped shoes were always purchased one or two sizes bigger to accommodate my cankles. Getting underwear was next to impossible too, unless I bought from the US. My usual descriptor was either 'big-boobed' or 'the fat one' which at any tone of voice, is hurtful to hear. Any time I was given a shirt to wear for an event, I needed to get it in advance so I could have panels added to the sides so it actually fit.

They were minor things, but things that annoyed me nonetheless. I try very hard not to let my personality revolve around my size. I wasn't sure if it was showing.

"Dad's on the phone with Tita Flora," Mags rolled her eyes as she picked up a stick. "She called just as the clock struck midnight, and they've been talking ever since."

I made a face. As much as we all loved Dad's oldest sister Flora, sometimes she didn't know what "time zones" meant. There was a 12-hour difference between California and Manila, meaning, the later she called, the later Dad could go to bed. She didn't mean any harm, I knew, but still. I wanted to go rescue him, but Bibi's sudden leap on to the couch for a snuggle and Maggie's pasalubong-expectant face made me stay.

I sighed and reached for my luggage, huffing loudly as I struggled to pull it next to me. My jeans weren't exactly the most comfortable, and it dug in to my stomach as I sat. I undid the button and…aaaah. Much better.

A couple more grunts later, my bag was open and the goodies spilled forth. I loved the look on Maggie's face when she's seen something particularly amazing. At eighteen, she was becoming less and less of a little girl, but that look of wonder was something she's had since she was a baby. I chewed on my banana-cues, going through the products with her.

"Oooh, is this lip liner?" She asked, holding up a slim, mauve box. It was the box of lip liner I went through three stores just to find. I nodded.

"Can I try it?"

"….sure," I said hesitantly as Maggie unscrewed the cap and swiped it across her lips. It looked so good on her that I said nothing as she added it to her personal pile.

Dad and I only managed to say hello after thirty minutes of Maggie exclaiming over the best that Korean cosmetics had to offer. He appeared in the doorway, giving us a stern look. As always, he held a steaming cup of barako coffee in his hands, the strongest coffee in the Philippines, as he proudly proclaimed. Dad enjoyed his coffee the same way every day—black and incredibly strong with a punch of sweetness from muscovado sugar.

"Girls," he said in an equally stern voice. A wrinkle appears between his eyebrows when he is particularly tired, and I could see it prominently now in the dim light of the hallway as well as I could see the curls of warmth coming out of the coffee cup. "Bed. Now. Mass tomorrow."

"But Daaaad," Maggie whined. "Makeup!"

"Bed," he repeated like Maggie wasn't already eighteen years old. I laughed as she begrudgingly headed off to her bedroom with her new makeup practically spilling out of her hands. I stopped laughing when I realized that Dad was also staring at me.

"What?" I asked innocently. He nodded his head and pointed his lips in the general direction of the bedrooms. I frowned and stood up from the couch, looking back at Bibi, who looked up at me, rolled backwards for a belly rub, and fell off the couch.

"Come on, dummy," I laughed, nudging my head and indicating for him to follow. I walked up to Dad to give him a quick peck on the cheek. "What did Tita Flora want?"

His face turned serious suddenly. I knew the question was a little blunt, but it was a little trick I did that let him know that I wanted to know so I could get annoyed.

"She's scheduling a flight back to Manila, her and Ate Fauna," he said, referring to Tita Flora's twin sister who had relocated to California at the behest of her sister. "She said she had something to tell us…not over the phone."

"Sounds serious," I said, biting my lip. My father nodded.

"Nothing I can do about it right now," he pointed out, sighing. "Oh, and Merry called too. She was looking for you. Something about an event she wanted to plan with you to raise funds for the Metropolitan Theatre. You know her and her pet projects," he shrugged, following me and Bibi up the steps.

"Oh no, Dad, you didn't say I would do that, did you?" I asked skeptically, raising an eyebrow at him.

Dad shrugged nonchalantly. Mom, Maggie, and I were always very vocal about our disapproval of Tita Merry's hold on Dad, but since he was the youngest brother to three overbearing sisters, he couldn't help it. He liked pointing out that his lot in life was being surrounded by wonderful, strong women. I wondered if that included me.

"She said she was looking for someone to plan it with her," he said as we reached the second floor. Bibi was already clawing at my bedroom door, begging to go inside. "Should I have volunteered you for the task?"

"Come now, don't tease," I said sarcastically, kissing his cheek again. "Night, Dad."

"Night," He said, smiling a little before squeezing one of the bulges of fat on my side. I yelped and he laughed all the way to his bedroom.

Bibi was already asleep by my bedroom door. I sighed and gently picked him up, feeling the uncomfortable four-hour flight take its toll on me.

I feel my sexiest when I'm lying in bed. My entire body feels flat and slim over my sheets, my limbs stretch all the way to the edges of the bed and I feel like I'm six feet tall. Sure, my massive boobs are practically pressing into my throat, which give me a bad case of double chin, but I didn't care. Sometimes, I close my eyes and picture myself beautiful and sexy, still curvy of course, but in the way that plus-sized models are curvy in all the right places.

Sometimes, I imagine a guy sleeping next to me, impossible as it seems. His face is unclear, like he's covered in pillows and sheets, but I know he's there. In my head he gazes at me adoringly every morning, even when I snore or when my face is squished against my pillows. Sometimes, I picture myself as one of those girls in coffee commercials, the ones who wear their guy's button down shirts to bed and look sexy and fresh. Then I chastise myself for being delusional and silly because the guy would have to wear a shirt thrice his size to fit me well.

And now I'm awake early on a Sunday.

I love Sundays just as much as the next person, but there is a laziness to it that makes me not want to get out of bed. My Sundays are for going to church, eating out for lunch, falling asleep for afternoon siesta, and enjoying a leisurely family dinner. It's tradition for Sundays to be about family, and I am usually diligent about that.

Either way, I was awake. Bibi was still asleep against me, burying his face in my rolls of fat. I rolled away in the other direction, immediately waking him up as I reached for my phone. After a few rings, he picked up.

"…hhhmmmph."

"You're not with anyone right now, are you?" I asked, lowering my voice.

"You can come over now, baby, she already left," he joked in a half-sleepy, half-sultry voice that was so deep it was disconcerting. Ugh. He loves making me uncomfortable, and he loves making jokes. I heard barking in the background and sheets being ruffled as they were tugged off his bed. It sounded like Wookie also wanted his human to wake up already.

"Was that Wookie?" I asked, petting Bibi's fur as my dog resumed snoozing.

"I knew it was a mistake getting a golden retriever," he grumbled, but it sounded like he was finally getting out of bed.

"Quit complaining and get dressed," I told him.

"Quit smothering me," he complained.

"Oh you love it," I teased. "See you at Mass, loser."

"See you, loser."

* * *

Ten minutes and a tapsilog breakfast later (the breakfast of champions!), we pulled up in front of the Padre Pio church for Mass. Max Angeles was already standing in the back of the church with his head bowed slightly as the service was going on.

He was dressed in his usual pair of slim, dark wash jeans, and his Dad's old Styx t-shirt. He loved wearing his shirts one size smaller, he once told me it was to get girls to focus on the muscles on his long, sinewy arms. I had to concede that it was one of his best features, the others being the long lashes shading his light brown eyes, and his chiseled jaw, if you're into that.

I called Max every Sunday to remind him to go to Mass with me. He was part-Chinese and very upper class, the kind whose family became rich in the last ten years, and the kind who didn't go to church except for Christmas and Easter.

Despite his net worth of approximately seven hundred million pesos (mostly in foreign investments, he'd shrugged when I found out), Max considered himself a pretty normal guy. He graduated from an international school in Manila before taking up Veterinary Medicine in

UP Los Baños. He could have easily gone abroad, but he wanted to stay in the Philippines "for the chicks."

It was a lie, of course, but he never liked talking about himself.

When he graduated, his parents migrated to the US, leaving him to live on his own in his condo unit in Ortigas to fend for himself. His only companions in life are Wookie, his large golden retriever, the maid that came in once a week to clean and do the laundry, and me, his best friend.

But Max is the kind of guy that needed to be constantly doing something, and the only time I ever see him sit still is when he's checking on his patients in his veterinary clinic or when he's reading a book. Max loves to read. It was common for me to see him finish one book and pick up another to start on straightaway. When we saw the last Harry Potter movie together, he finally admitted that he had wanted to be a vet because of Hagrid, the hairy half-giant who was forever keeping strange pets.

Right now he was reading through Jonathan Tropper's This Is Where I Leave You which I slowly realized was the reason why his head was bowed low.

"Dude!" I exclaimed, slapping his arm as soon as I managed to walk up to him. I winced as my toes complained. This is what I get for wearing heels to regular Sunday mass.

He looked up in confusion as Maggie giggled at him, and my mother gave his book a sharp look. Dad just looked sympathetic at his dilemma before they went deeper into the church to get seats. "Are you seriously reading during the homily?"

Max and I were like the Doctor and Donna Noble, best friends, partners, and equals with a strict "no mating" policy in effect. We met two years ago at a Pet Training Class he taught as a summer job out of boredom.

In the class, Bibi learned to sit, stay, and to recognize his name. I found a best friend in Max. I asked him for help with Bibi's behavior on the first day, and he asked if I wanted lunch before I could open my mouth.

The next thing I knew, the class was over and we were in each other's lives. We liked the same movies, the same TV shows, and listened to the same local bands. He read all the books I wished I had read, and regaled me with stories of his dating disasters.

Unfortunately for him, being his best friend also involved me happily smothering him with my care, making sure that he attended Mass with me on Sundays, that he had food in his condo, and that Wookie isn't left sitting by a bench while his human is distracted by a book.

"Well, I was until you showed up," he said pointedly, folding the edge of the page to make sure he didn't get lost in his reading before he closed the book. He leaned in and gave me his usual friendly kiss on the cheek. "Welcome back by the way, gorgeous."

I looked up at him just in time to catch him smiling at me. He was already tapping his foot impatiently on the floor.

"I missed you," he said. "I missed your nagging."

Max has always had an adorable smile, one that was half-mischievous and half-smug. It made him a fantastic liar, and it was one of the things that I like about him. I'd told him many times that he'd be a great con artist.

"Flattery won't get you anywhere," I nudged the side of his stomach with my elbow and he guffawed, eliciting a withering glare from one of the more strict churchgoers. I smiled sheepishly as an apology and turned to face the altar. What was the priest talking about? Something about being nice to your neighbors or something…

"Did you get me pasalubong?" He asked. "Presents, presents, my kingdom for presents! I seem to remember I asked for a Korean sex gong."

"No," I replied curtly, keeping my eyes up front. "Focus on the Mass."

He started swaying a bit while he stood. I elbowed him again.

"By the way," I whispered. "Koreans don't have sex gongs. Believe me, I asked."

I felt my cheeks burning as Max started laughing. I knew it! I knew he was just baiting me with that! I asked exactly three stores at Insadong before I managed to work out that Max was having a laugh from thousands of miles away. I would never forget the bewildered looks the Korean salesladies gave me when I tried to describe the said gong.

Max was still laughing, and the same woman that had glared at us earlier was now pursing her lips, ready to tell him off. I pulled his arm and led him to the bathrooms until his laughter subsided. At this rate we were going to be kicked out of the church!

"Will you stop?" I asked, crossing my arms, and glaring at him. I quickly realized that I was sweating, thanks to the heat of the summer and the blush from embarrassment on my cheeks. I took a couple of quick breaths and tried to cool down so I didn't look like a big round tomato in my equally red dress. I leaned against the bathroom sink, easily accepting Max's hand as he helped me sit on the marble countertop. He was still laughing.

"You're impossible," I grumbled at him. He stopped laughing just to wink exaggeratedly at me, handing me a piece of tissue which he'd run under the sink to help cool my face. If I didn't find it so funny I knew I would have slapped his arm again. I dabbed the tissue against my skin.

"That's why I have you to keep me in line, Martha," he said, giving me a quick little wink before pulling at my hand to get me off of the bathroom counter. I'm always a little embarrassed that he has to help me sometimes, but if he minded, Max never mentioned it. I tossed the used tissue into the nearby trash bin. "Now can we go back? You really have to learn to behave when attending Mass."

I slapped his arm again and he scowled in fake pain while we made our way back to our spot by the doors. The man was impossible, but I loved him anyway.

two

One of my least favorite things about coming home from a trip is the inevitable realization that you're back to your usual routines. After spending a week in the utter bliss of having a relaxed schedule, waking up early to go to work is the worst. The worst-iest worst. Especially when you check your phone first thing in the morning to see that you've already got three text messages waiting for your immediate response.

> Martha hija, good morning! Did you have a good breakfast? I quite enjoyed mine since Yaya served the dried fish we got from that weekend market—you know, the same one your mother likes to visit sometimes. Was she there? I don't think I saw her.

That was the first text. My aunt, Merryweather Aguas-Benitez, texted like she talked, and she loved talking. It made asking her simple questions utterly impossible, which was why people thought she was fascinating and eccentric. Thankfully, she got to the point by her second message.

> I am so glad your Papa recommended you to help me for the Met Theatre fundraiser! This is already our second benefit together, and my friends in the arts are thrilled that we can create these things. Speaking of which, how are the invitations coming along? Did you speak to the printer?

Ah, yes. So I ended up helping her out with the fundraiser anyway, getting in touch with the printers first thing in that morning. Dad knew the magic words to use to get me into the project, which was that the event was soon, and "in dire need of my help."

Tita Merry's idea was actually very cool—a movie screening to raise funds to help restore the old Metropolitan Theatre in Manila. She wanted it to be a full experience, with décor, people in costumes, theme food, and a live band to play the score.

Tita Merry was always up to things like this. Ever since Tito Gerund Benitez, the shipping magnate, died two years ago, Tita Merry kept herself busy with charity events, gallery openings, and art sponsorships, making good use of her now considerable fortune.

This fundraiser was only one of many she had already passed on to me. This meant that I already knew the drill. Invitations three weeks before, then two weeks for coordination with the designers, one week for set-up until the event. She already had a list of invitees and contacts for everything, so I didn't think it was going to be too hard.

Plus, I get to pick the movie and the theme! I was still debating between The Sound of Music and Clue. Both would require a lot of work thematically, but when done right, would make the evening memorable.

To be perfectly honest, I liked doing these events. They took up a lot of my time, but it was always rewarding to know that I could do something to help.

Yes Tita, picking them up on Wednesday after work, I texted back.

That is wonderful! Come over later so we can discuss. Mrs. Aquino next door brought ensaymada and tsokolate from her farm so we can have those.

I had to admit, Tita Merry really knew how to feed people. I smacked my lips in anticipation of the soft, sweet buns with sharp cheese baked on top and the warm, creamy hot chocolate made from pressed cocoa. Knowing how to feed people was a Filipino art form Tita Merry had mastered very well. I set the appointment with her, making a mental note to let Benjo know where to pick me up before I moved on to the next message.

MAJOR WORK EMERGENCY I AM HAVING A BREAKDOWN HERE

I frowned at the message. Where Tita Merry loved length to her texts, my officemate Mindy Capras loved to text in all caps. She was a certified drama queen, in her words, but texting me at 8am was unlike her. She often remarked that she only became an accountant to fund lavish clothes and her crazy expensive gym membership. Bare minimum was her style, according to her.

Calm down, I responded. *Text details. On the way there.*

I sent off the quick reply and headed straight for the shower. I'd be ready to go in thirty minutes. This was what I did in the office. I was a problem-solver, which worked well with my inherent need to help people. Everyone knew that "I need you" was my weakness. It was a symptom of the lonely.

I hummed a little tune to myself as I looked into my closet. I pulled out a pair of wide leg trousers I paid a little too much for at H&M, then a silk button down shirt that was a men's size XXL. I was sure it was going to look fantastic with my favorite camel heels.

I loved dressing up, and I did my research. I read all the books, blogs and beauty bibles, kept myself updated on the rules and made up my own.

Over time, I learned to love dressing for my body, wearing heels and short skirts like it was nobody's business. When the outfit was right, I felt like I could take over the world. When the outfit was wrong…I didn't even like thinking about when the outfit was wrong.

I had quite a nice shape when you looked at me straight-on. Then there were the usual observations—my gigantic breasts, my bulging belly (and the lovely stretch marks that accompanied it), my Michelin man arms and tree trunk legs. I loved and accepted my body parts most of the time, but there were one or two moments in the day when I would close my eyes and hope that everything was actually smaller than it looked.

Bibi barked to get my attention. I turned to him and saw that he was giving me that look, one that seemed constantly amazed at how a mess like me managed to keep him alive.

Or maybe he was bored.

"Hey boy," I said, smiling as I picked up his favorite toy from where we left it under the bed. "Who wants to play?"

He perked up immediately, wagging his tail and running around the floor. I raised the toy and tossed it…just for it to hit him in the face when he jumped up to catch it.

"Aww Bibi," I laughed, coming over to pick him up. "I know how you feel."

* * *

Mindy's response came in after my shower. Apparently one of our consulting meetings was bumped up from Friday to today, and she had nothing ready. I coached her though the phone, trying to help her gather enough of the materials before I got in to polish her presentation. I explained to her what the client was looking for, and that managed to calm her down somewhat. Thank god. Mindy had been my assistant for about seven months now, and she wasn't used to the more erratic pace of our foreign clientele yet.

I work in an accounting firm where investors came to us and ask how they can create, improve on, or generate investments in the Philippines. We help them with their registrations and filings, but we do a lot of advising and hand-holding too. It's a one-stop shop kind of place to help investors navigate the landmine that is Philippine business. I loved it, but sometimes the pace was demanding, and half the time I felt like I had no idea what I was doing.

"Marta-martita!" Ellen singsonged from downstairs. "Time to go! Your Papa is waiting downstairs!"

Shoot. I gave myself one last glance in the mirror and twisted my hair into a quick topknot.

Hello gorgeous, I told myself. I smiled at my reflection and headed off to work.

* * *

"Is it possible to only half-love yourself?" I asked Max over the phone three hours later. What should have been an hour-long drive to the office (even with traffic) actually took two hours. Our driver Benjo tried to take a shortcut but ended up in a lane with a traffic accident blocking up the main highway. Safe to say my mood hadn't really improved. Not even the grande caramel macchiato and pearl sugar waffle I got from Starbucks was helping.

Thankfully, Mindy's presentation was ready to go, just in time for the client to arrive at the office. I was supposed to be making a competitive analysis of two franchise opportunities when I had the feeling that I should call Max.

"Martha, I'm not going to lie," he said from his end of the line. "I have no idea what you're talking about. But if you're talking about love, I am an expert in the subject."

"I'm pretty sure we're talking about a different kind of love. But I'm talking about self-love."

"What, now? In the office?"

"MAX! Ugh, never mind!" I said with a sigh. "This heat is just getting me down. Plus it was total carmageddon from Ortigas to Makati. You're lucky it only takes you a ten-minute walk to get to the clinic."

"In forty-degree heat with my fragile porcelain skin?" He laughed. "Yeah, I'm lucky."

"That's why I bought you a hat, Max! You're supposed to wear it!"

To most people, Max was Doc Max, a veterinarian with his own clinic in the fancy mini mall in front of the compound of his fancy condominium. Running the clinic and seeing his patients kept him busy most days and it wasn't unusual for him to be answering texts or giving soothing words of advice to his patients over the phone.

"I'm actually in the car too."

"Liar liar," I chanted, taking a small bite off of my waffle. Pearl sugar bits, yum!

"I shit you not! I met this woman at a bar last night. She's moving back to Cebu this afternoon so I'm on a crazy rush to the airport to win her hand in marriage."

"Max, I'm not really in the mood for your imaginary sexcapades."

He must have sensed the annoyance in my voice, because he laughed it off to lighten my mood. "I'm on my way to Manila Zoo. One of my old college classmates is doing a giraffe birth, and I'm assisting."

I frowned, trying to discern if he was telling the truth.

"I don't know much about your job, but I do know your specialization is dogs and cats," I pointed out. I remembered because he explained to me once at length why he was jealous of the hundred-year old man in a book for having an elephant he couldn't possibly be certified to take care of. "Are you certified?"

"Well, it's a birth, so it's mainly just catching the calf when it comes out," he joked, making me roll my eyes slightly. "Hey, cheer up, will you? The sun is shining, you're eating a Starbucks waffle—"

"How did you know that I—"

"I'm bringing a baby giraffe into this—SHIT!"

There was a sound of car tires screeching to a halt and Max likely slamming on his horn. I jerked up in my seat, not really sure why. It wasn't as if I could go to Max right now.

"Everything okay?" I asked, as he honked his horn one more time.

"Just the usual driving hazards," He sighed. "We need to play hooky one day, Martha. Just you, me, *Ang Bandang Shirley* and the highway, that's all I want in life."

Max's enthusiasm was always infectious, and I knew from experience that he loved taking long drives with his favorite songs playing in the background.

"It would never work out, you love your pet patients too much to totally disconnect," I said, fighting the urge to smile. His idea was actually really nice. Maybe we did need a day to just get away from it all. Maybe.

"I know. Plus I'm actually excited about this giraffe birth. I even downloaded a GPS app for the drive," he pointed out proudly, and this time it was my turn to get excited. Max was slightly old school in some ways. He loved local bands, so all he listened to were CDs. He had social media accounts, but never used it on his phone (too busy with patients, he said). Twitter bored him, Instagram was way too "hipster" for him, and Goodreads just "spoiled the surprise."

"Thank god!" I exclaimed. "How is it working out so far?"

"Well, I've had to drive through a couple of sketchy areas where there were more people than street, but so far so good."

"Just keep your doors locked and your windows up and you should be fine," I advised. "Do you have water? It's really hot out, and the Manila Zoo isn't exactly air conditioned."

"Yes Mommy," he teased. He paused. "I'm wearing that stupid baseball cap you got me. Feeling better now?"

"Much," I told him. I know that right then, I should have said "'thank you for making me feel better" or "you're the best-est friend a big girl could have." But Max already knew these things. I never really had to tell him, which was one of the best parts of our friendship. All I could really say was, "Try not to get giraffe placenta on you."

"I won't."

"Bye," I chirped.

"Byeeeee," He said, letting the 'eee' ring out until he hung up. I was still smiling when Mindy came back from her presentation, a knowing look on her face as she balanced the projector, her laptop and the clients' financial statements in her arms.

"Whooo was thaaaat?" She asked in a singsong voice, swaying her body in time to her singsong as she set her baggage down before she turned on me. "Waaaas iiit a booooy?"

I scoffed, resuming my work. What was I supposed to be doing again? Oh right, competitive analysis. "It was just Max."

"Uh-huh," Mindy said, like I just told her everything she needed to know.

"By the way," she continued, picking up the projector carefully to return to the IT department. "Shelly's in there with the clients, and they asked for you because they wanted a discount on the retainer agreement. I would go in there before Shelly loses her nerve and freaks."

Right, time to work.

I headed to the conference room, ready to be all smiles and coquettish laughs when my eyes immediately zoned in on a familiar face in the group. Suddenly a two hundred pound stone dropped in my stomach me, my legs wobbled in my heels, and I wanted to cover up my stomach with my hands. My heart hammered in my chest and my palms actually started to sweat.

And all because I saw Enzo Miguel again.

God, even his name is so cool. He and I were orgmates in college, both of us sharing a passion for musical theatre. I was usually relegated to the chorus because there weren't a lot of characters for my body type, but Enzo was always, always cast as the leading man. He had the most handsome face, with a sharp angled chin and a straight, pointed nose. His eyes were on the small, chinky side, but his grin was so sexy I swear to God it made a girl faint once.

Then there was his hair. It was always perfectly styled, like he had been cast in a shampoo commercial. He wasn't the tallest guy in the room, but he just filled it with such energy that everyone was drawn to him like moons to a planet.

Exhibit A, me, quite possibly the biggest moon there was.

I took small, quick breaths as I neared the room. The clients were already starting to notice me, as people usually did from a mile away.

Keep calm, keep calm. Martha Aguas, get your head together! It's no big deal. It's just Enzo. You haven't spoken to him in years, and you haven't heard from him since…since…

"Hello," I managed to say, peeking into the conference room. I looked at Shelly, the finance officer, first. It was important that I recognized her as the one conducting the meeting. "Hey Shell, I'm really sorry. Mindy asked me to step in. Is there anything I can do?"

"Oh yes," Shelly said, and I could tell from the look she gave me that she actually meant to say "oh yes!" She immediately ushered me in, even when all I wanted to do was hide away and blush. My heart simply refused to calm down.

"Martha," A familiar voice said from the opposite side of the room. "Nice to see you again."

I refocused and smiled before I could register who it was. But when I saw her, my grin only got wider.

"Ava!" I said, crossing the room to buss my friend's cheek. "You're back from Bali! Did you get to stay in that place in Seminyak?"

Ava Bonifacio was one of my classmates in college, and one of the smartest people I knew. She was the lady with a plan, working as a paralegal for the law firm that referred clients to our company. About a week ago she'd called me in a panic, asking if I knew any decent place in Bali to stay. I hadn't even known that she was on vacation. I immediately noticed that she was much tanner now, and one of her buttons were undone. I had never seen her like that before.

"Oh, no, I ended up staying in Sudamala," she said. Was she...oh my, she was actually blushing. What on earth happened to her in Bali?

"We'll talk about it later," she said to me.

"Gotcha," I said, winking at her. We sometimes met up for dinner when she was free, and I didn't mind that we talked mostly about work. Something was different now, though. I wondered what it was. I turned to the other people in the room.

As with most business meetings, everyone stood up when I crossed the room to say hi to Ava. She took over the introductions as I shook hands and smiled at unfamiliar faces. Enzo was sitting at the back, so we weren't introduced. But I did throw him a tiny, knowing smile. I wondered if he recognized me. Did he work with Ava? Was he the reason for her tan skin and undone button?

I smiled at the group. I was practiced in the art of acting like I didn't see him, and the practice was put to excellent use now. It was totally possible that he had no idea who I was--I mean, in every sense of the term, I was just a background character to him.

"Gentlemen," Ava said, addressing the group. For the benefit of those who I hadn't met before, she must have felt an introduction was proper. "This is Martha Aguas."

Eyes widened at Ava's revelation. Interestingly enough, the company name was right behind my head, so the connection was quickly made. I worked at Aguas, Gatchalian & Partners, CPAs, which just so happened to be my father's company.

"Oh, you're Philip's daughter!" Frank, our client, exclaimed, extending his hand for me to shake again. I had already met him last week when he was first introduced to my father, and I actually arranged this meeting for him. "You introduced yourself as his assistant at the meeting last time, I had no idea."

I smiled and got ready to launch into my usual joke. I liked diffusing my self-imposed tensions with a joke.

"Well if he had his way he would introduce me as his little dumpling," I joked, chuckling.

"Ah yes, of course of course!" Frank laughed, nodding his agreement. Then he looked me up and down, taking in every bit of me. I assumed that he was trying to find similarities between myself and my father, surprising everyone in the room when he exhaled and said. "You're such a…healthy young lady! Your father must work a lot to feed you, eh?"

The room burst into polite laughter, and I tried, I really tried not to let it get to me. This wasn't exactly the first time a client made unsolicited comments about my weight. I was a professional, after all. I swallowed down the flash of annoyance, my embarrassment, and pride before I gave the richest, rudest man in the room a smile. I saw Ava flinch for me in the corner, but maintained the smile.

"Hm. Is there anything I can help you with?" I asked instead, shrugging it off. I was under no illusion that I was the sexiest woman in the room, but that didn't give anyone the right to speak to me that way. Through experience, I've learned that these incidents were best swept under the rug before they became a big deal. While insensitive comments hurt, it was better not to say anything, just so the person who said them didn't feel like I thought they were funny, clever, or cool.

At least that was what I said when I was at work.

"Yes, your retainer," Frank's assistant spoke up, brandishing the statement Shelley had my father approve yesterday. "Quite frankly, it's a bit too expensive for us, if it's just consulting and auditing. We're getting our own accountants, our own books."

"Oh, of course," I said. "May I see the retainer agreement?"

The agreement was passed to me, and I quickly scanned the terms and fees Shelly prepared. I didn't need to see it, really. I came here with the express purpose of explaining why we couldn't give them a discount. My father liked to think that once you gave in, they would always ask, and lower the value of our advice. It wasn't because the guy basically made a sexist fat joke directed at me.

"I'm really sorry, Frank," I said with a tiny sigh. "This agreement is pretty standard for clients. I can assure you that the prices will be the same for any other firm of good standards. Now if you could excuse me, gentlemen, I need to go back to the office. Ava, I'll see you later?"

"I'll text you," she said, already texting me an apology with her free hand.

I walked out of the conference with a confident smile, almost completely forgetting that Enzo was there, and craving a large peppermint milk tea in the middle of my rage.

> Ava: I'm sorry about them. Let's have dinner and I can charge it to them

I snorted. Ava was so straight-laced, just the suggestion of her charging a client for a casual dinner was hilarious. I headed straight for the milk tea place downstairs while responding to her text and gave in, sipping boba from their largest cup like a vacuum. I tried calling Max, but all I got back was him yelling 'OH GOD IS THAT THE LEGS' before he accidentally hung up.

> Ava: Hope you're not too upset.

Of course I was livid, and I was hurt. Sometimes people just say things to you without really thinking about how that affected you, and this was how Frank had affected me. The sweet, slightly minty milk tea filled something inside me that had been drained out at his little joke. Like I was building my bravery and confidence reserve again. It felt satisfying, even if at the back of my mind I knew that it was only temporary.

"May I join you?" A voice asked.

"Sure, whatever," I said dismissively, looking away.

"Martha?"

"What," I said, still not looking.

"Ah. So it is you," the voice said, and realization slowly started to dawn on me. I turned my head, inch by inch, daring myself not to hope that I was right. "I wasn't sure, I didn't think…You don't remember me, do you?"

It was him, really him! All five feet six inches of him, with the same smile and the same floppy black hair. Enzo sat across from me, and if I was brave I could reach out with my hand and touch his with minimal effort. He'd loosened his tie at some point, which made him more real, and more like his old self. I smiled.

"Oh come on, Enzo," I said nonchalantly. "Would I forget you?"

Saying his name felt special, like a secret that I'd been keeping to myself for so long. I didn't even realize how hard I had crushed on him until that moment. He smiled, and all was right in the world again. His hand, which was resting on the small linoleum table, flexed slightly. I had a sudden flash of memory about that hand on my body, its warmth making me shiver. I never forgot the way that hand molded my flesh beneath it, while his lips touched mine. It was ages ago, and I shouldn't be having these hot memory flashes, but there they were, fresh like they were made yesterday.

"Martha," He said, suddenly serious. "I'm really sorry about Frank. I don't exactly work for him because of his tact."

"It's okay," I said, finally turning to face him, my milk tea cup completely empty. "I wouldn't last long in my job if I let things like that get to me." I guiltily tossed the cup to the trash can. If I was going to make polite conversation with an old crush (and I knew he was much more than that), I was going to do it right and take control of the conversation. "So you work with Ava?"

He didn't miss a beat. "No, I'm Frank's local liaison, a fancy term for the guy that introduces him to other guys and makes things happen. I saw Ava's posts on Facebook and remembered she worked at a law firm, which led me here."

"Ah," I said, not even asking how he knew Ava. We were all from the same university anyway, it was a small world. "So aside from working for a startup, how are you? I think the last time I saw you was..."

I thought back to the last time I saw him, and my heart clenched involuntarily in my chest. The last time I saw him was at the cast party for the university production of *Hairspray*, the only play I was chosen to be principal in, because I was a senior and the only one that fit the big and beautiful Tracy Turnblad body type. Enzo was naturally cast as my Link Larkin.

I didn't really approach him before, dismissing him as a handsome, douchebag type that boys from his high school usually were, but he proved me wrong. He started making jokes, singing really obscure theatre songs for sound check, running lines and steps with me, helping me out when I got lost.

By opening night I was so in love with him that the director told me to "save my googley love eyes for the next show." Things didn't really escalate between us until the night of the cast party, when he announced he was flying to London to go to drama school.

At the office cafeteria, I saw him swallow thickly, his other thumb tucked lightly into his belt to adjust it. I knew he was thinking about that night too.

My friends had been getting boyfriends and losing their virginity left and right. He was leaving, I was probably never going to see him again, so I took a deep breath, looked at Enzo and said, "listen, everyone's doing it, and I just want to get it over and done with, so can we?"

Miraculously, he'd agreed. So while everyone got drunk at the cast party, he and I engaged in very awkward (and I'm talking teeth smashing, "where is that supposed to go" and a lot of drunk giggling) but very safe sex.

It was my first, and his too. My desire to jump over this particular milestone was so insistent that I barely remembered how the act itself felt. I mostly remembered him, the way he wanted me to slow down, how his hands fumbled over the condom. I remembered him kissing me. Him smiling when I could not stop telling him how he was making me feel.

Lying in his bed afterward, both of us wide-eyed and panting like we couldn't believe it, I didn't feel much of the satisfaction I hoped I would feel. I knew it wasn't going to go beyond that night, and it broke my heart worse than his rejection would have.

So while he was asleep, I kissed his cheek and wished him luck.

Years later, he sat across me in a corporate building, looking so formal in his slacks and shirt, I wanted to take back asking him what happened.

"The cast party for *Hairspray*," he suddenly said, like he didn't remember what happened between us at all. "You were wearing a white dress with gold things on the sleeves," he demonstrated by waving his fingers over his taut shoulders.

"You remember that?" I ask, taken aback.

"Well...yeah," He said like it was no big deal at all. "I remember everything."

For no apparent reason, my breath caught in my throat. I had no idea what to make of that, and for the second time that day, I was left reeling. His cell phone started to ring, and I didn't miss Frank's name flashing on the screen. He sighed and picked it up.

"Hi, Frank," he said quickly, casting me a quick glance like I was being asked after. "I just stepped out. Yes I will meet you at the lobby. Five minutes? Okay."

Then he hung up, his brows slightly furrowed in concern.

"Trouble in paradise?" I asked, trying to be just a little bit more casual than I felt. Enzo gave a little laugh. You see, that was a casual office joke.

"You could say that," He said. He reached over the table and looked right at my face. It was the same look he had on stage, when he was trying to make a girl fall in love with him. I wondered if he knew he was doing it.

"Martha," he said, "I really want to catch up with you."

I didn't know I was raising my eyebrows until he laughed.

"I'm serious! Look, maybe we could exchange numbers?"

A strange thrill ran through my body, from the tips of my toes to the ends of our almost touching fingers. Inside I was screaming, "Yes yes, a thousand times yes!" while my fingers were fumbling for my phone.

We exchanged numbers, and he gave me a friendly kiss on the cheek.

"You look fantastic by the way," he said. "Did you lose weight?"

"Ha-ha, very funny, Mister Charming," I said, rolling my eyes at him. "Don't you have a boss to attend to?"

"Right, right. Sorry. Text me later?" He asked, and I nodded.

A smile, a wave, a turn and then he was gone. I collapsed against the crappy plastic chair, almost forgetting to be careful in case it gave out. My cheeks were burning, my heart was hammering in my chest, and my fingers were shaking slightly. I felt like I'd swallowed a thousand butterflies brewing a storm in my sizeable stomach. I'd acted out this feeling so many times in college, but the actual emotion still caught me by surprise.

It was plain, unadulterated kilig. It rose up like fizz in a soda can, the bubbles popping in my heart. But as soon as they did, my heart sank to the pit of my stomach.

The last time I felt this way was years ago, when I lay in bed with Enzo and knew that I was in love with him, and he was never going to love me back.

He was the last thing I needed right now, but I didn't want to let him go

Three

The next thing I knew, it was three weeks later, and the day of Tita Merry's screening for the Metropolitan Theatre. I skipped work that day to make sure everything was ready for the event.

I had chosen *Clue*, an offbeat, slightly eccentric movie based on the board game, with a lot of fun alternate endings and a murder to boot. I'd spent the last three weeks getting costumes for Mrs. White, Miss Scarlett, Mrs. Peacock, Mr. Green, Colonel Mustard, etc., and picking out items that could have fit in scary old Boddy Mansion on a stormy night.

We were holding the screening in one of the fancy theatres at one of the many malls in Manila. We built temporary dividers in the lobby to recreate the rooms in the game, and put in all the fun things in the room where people can play games, leave donations and generally have a great time.

So I spent the last two nights making so much fake blood that my hands were still slightly red, even though I was not being paid for any of this. But anything for family, right?

Before I descended into the chaos of the setup at the venue (I had to go earlier than planned because Tita Merry was incommunicado for some weird reason), I had breakfast at Max's condo. As awesome as it was having him so close to my place, I hated going there. The buildings looked so alike I could hardly tell one apart from the other. And I say this only because I get lost each time I go. Sure he had all of these cool amenities and businesses close by and the lobby was worthy of a five-star hotel, but I just couldn't imagine putting my life in a box that was exactly the same as everyone else's.

Plus, his hallway was just as impossible. The only way I knew which apartment was Max's was because I tacked an old Grimace sticker to his door one day, and he never bothered to remove it. Thank god for purple amorphous beings from fast food joints.

Max's place had two main pieces of furniture. First was the floor to ceiling bookshelf he had specially made to house his collection. Second was his super cool, high tech sound system for all his music. Our best afternoons were spent in his house, listening to music with the dogs on our laps while Max read and I tripped over the books he forgot to put away.

Like right now, when I knocked over a pile of books trying to get to his closet. He never seemed to mind, but I did. There's nothing like having a 50-inch waist and having to wriggle through tight spaces to make you uncomfortable. We were listening to Trainman, which is at the top of Max's favourite bands. He loved their music so much that we actually flew to Japan once for a music festival just to see them perform.

"Max, how do you ever get girls in here?" I exclaimed, nearly tripping over one of the many piles of books on the floor while Nevermind, his current favorite, played.

We had just had breakfast at a pie place downstairs, and now I was trying to find him a nice shirt for the screening tonight. I don't usually choose his clothes for him, but if I was going to throw Max into the firing squad (aka Tita Merry), he might as well be prepared. "You have books on every empty space on the floor!"

"The women I take back to my condo are only interested in one piece of furniture," Max pointed out, sitting on the floor with Wookie sprawled over his legs. He pursed his lips towards the surprisingly neatly-made bed, which made me roll my eyes and resume my trudge towards his closet.

I could feel him watching me behind his glasses. His eyesight was horrible, and he usually wore contacts to keep 'looking foxy' when he went out, but wore glasses when he was at home. He was holding a copy of *The Goldfinch*. His foot shook and tapped against the window frame.

He absently ran a hand through his longish black hair. I keep telling him to get it cut and to shave the little beard he was cooking up, but to no avail. I showed Mindy a picture once and she said it only made him look twice as sexy—not that I noticed.

"I don't know how with shirts like these!" I said, pulling out a cherry red shirt that had 'Kiss Me, I'm Scottish!' in faded pink letters. It was cheeky but it also said, 'fancy a fuck?' on the back.

"I got that in Scotland from a friend, it's supposed to be funny!" He said, as Wookie raised his head, looked at the t-shirt and replaced his head on Max's lap, wiggling his nose.

"See, see, Wookie agrees with me!" I argued, shaking my head before resuming my digging. "It's unfair that you've been to Europe, and all you got was this lame shirt."

"I gained a wealth of experience too, thanks," he chuckled. "Aw, don't worry Martha! You and I are going there one day. We pinky-promised."

I pouted slightly, knowing how much value there was in Max Angeles's pinky promises. But it was something I've always wanted to do, go to Europe. I wanted to sit café side in Paris, to watch West End musicals in London and sample chocolates from Switzerland. I wanted to hear Bach played in a church in Prague, to yell at Italians while making weird hand gestures. The idea popped into my head when I was thirteen, when I realized being a supermodel was out of the question for me.

Since then I've been planning the perfect trip, the details of which Max helped me with since he's been going to Europe since he was a teenager. We had a route that took us from London to Paris, Paris to Switzerland and down to Italy and Spain. That was all I had so far, and already I was too excited for my own good.

But until I had enough money saved up, it was never going to happen. Plus my parents would only let me go if I brought Max with me to keep me safe. As if Max would be any good in a fistfight!

"I've seen you look decent before Maxwell, you have to work with me here," I said, changing the subject entirely so I didn't dwell on a trip that I couldn't take. Yet.

He shuddered at my use of his full name, as always.

"Hey, did you ever talk to that guy again?" He asked, and the long pause before he spoke again was indicative of his apprehension about the topic he was trying to bring up. He had been since I first mentioned it to him. "That theatre guy who wanted to 'catch up' with you."

"Oh, Enzo?" I asked breezily, unable to help the little thrill that made my shoulders rise and my breath catch when I talked about him. I was still in love with him, in a horrible, please-stop-taking-my-soul kind of way. I had been content to burn at a distance, trying to move on and forget. But he came back, and my heart ached for him again. I was so used to it that I wore it like a chip on my shoulder.

The reason why I told Max about it (and all he said was 'high five, man!' for me losing my virginity) was because I wanted to get it out of me and get it over with. Apparently I was wrong about that.

"Yes, that Enzo," he said, rolling his eyes like he could see the emotions vibrating off of me.

"What about him?" I asked, tossing a pair of pants to the bed.

"Don't beat around the bush, buddy," He said, putting his book down. "Did he 'catch up with you'?" he asked, making little air quotes with his fingers. I stared at him blankly. "It's a sex euphemism."

"I KNOW."

"Or did he never call you back?"

"We're texting," I said, trying to keep calm. "It's really nice. And we had a cup of coffee once or twice. We never talked about that night. We're just friends, Max. It's not like it's going anywhere."

From the dubious look on his face, I knew he could tell that I didn't really think that. Enzo and I have been texting a lot over the last three weeks. He liked texting random things, striking up conversations with me, asking what I was doing or if I'd seen one of the latest musicals Philippine theatre had to offer. It was nice to have someone to geek out with over musicals and about the people we used to know. We never really talked about how he came from theatrical glory to the corporate set-up, but it didn't really matter to me. I needed him at a distance so I wouldn't do anything stupid.

I went into the closet to try to find a shirt without giving Max another glance. That was when he pushed himself off of the floor and followed me into his dark and tiny walk-in closet. Wookie too, was pushing his damp nose against my leg.

"What the hell are you doing!" I shrieked, almost falling backwards, but Max caught my hand quickly. He reached behind me and pulled out a shirt. It felt luxurious and expensive in my hands, and in the light of his bedroom, actually looked very nice.

"There, shirt." He said gruffly.

Something I said put him in a bad mood. I didn't really have time to process it, though, because my phone started ringing. I dashed off to the living room where I left it, hitting my side against a table end. I yelled out in pain but continued my trek to my phone.

"Hellooooo?" I asked, grabbing my phone just as Wookie came over to check on me. I ended up slightly wheezing on Max's living room couch with his dog snuggling up against me in the middle of a heat wave. The poor guy was panting too.

"Martha?" The voice asked. "Oh Maaaartha?"

I gasped and my stomach clenched. I knew that voice.

"Regina?"

Deep, throaty laugher drifted in from her end of the phone line. I've known that voice since I was a little girl, since it was the same laugh that followed every horrible childhood taunt I received.

There was no mistaking it over the phone. Regina Benitez was calling me.

Regina was Tita Merry's only daughter, and my favorite (take note, only) cousin. She, Maggie, and I grew up together, swimming in rivers (where she tried to drown me), running in our undies through our grandparents' gardens (where she tripped me) when it rained. We even used to wear matching outfits (she would pull the bow out of my braid).

She moved to London after college for a master's degree in Art Management, and I hadn't heard from her since.

"You better believe it! I'm back!" She chanted over the phone. "I can't wait to bully you again! You remember how I would pinch you and call you Massive Martha?"

I didn't notice Max walking in to the living room as I rolled my eyes. The number of times I had cried over the word 'massive' was all because of an eleven-year old who thought it was funny to call her cousin fat.

"Yeah," I said dryly. "It was after you first went to London, and your mom was so proud you learned a new word."

A thought suddenly occurred to me. If Regina was back, then did that mean…

"I'll see you for that screening tonight," she said like she was lecturing me. "It's such a hassle. I heard Mama invited the Aguas clan to the thing."

I furrowed my brows in confusion. When Regina talked about the clan, she was talking about the whole Aguas Clan, consisting of the three matriarchs of the family, my Lola May, and her sisters April and June, and her children, and their children's children, which meant there were at least fifty other people coming to the event that I didn't know about. Tita Merry never added them to the invitations list, and she never mentioned that there was anything happening beyond the screening.

"Uh-huh," I said, already crossing one arm over my massive chest and frowning. "See you."

"See you, Massive Martha!"

Then she hung up.

"WHY do you have to be in my liiiiiffe," I groaned to my phone as I tossed it to the couch. Wookie disappeared from my side to rejoin his owner, and I turned to face Max already dressed in the outfit I had chosen for him.

The event wasn't formal, but I made sure he dressed up from his usual look. He wore the deep blue gingham button down I approved for him, which showed off the light tan in his skin from his day at the zoo. His dark beard was growing out slightly and full on his chin, which he brushed experimentally with a hand as he showed off the sinews on his arms. His shirt was tucked into the same slim cut pants I'd seen him wearing in church, the day he finished reading *This is Where I Leave You*, and secured with a tan belt. He was wearing a pair of pale blue socks with cute sheep leaping across them, my present to him from Seoul. I smiled at my friend, and he smiled back.

"God, I keep forgetting that you actually look gorgeous when you clean up," I said, pulling my charger from the plug as Wookie sniffed around it. I pat his head and sat back on the couch just to look at Max again.

"You looked annoyed," he said.

"My childhood tormenter is coming to the screening tonight. She seemed…eager to see me," I said, crinkling my nose. "And my aunt isn't answering her phone."

"Do you need help?"

"Nah, I'm good. Letting me dress you is all the help you can give," I chuckled.

"Let me rephrase then. What can I do for you in way of sustenance, gorgeous?" he asked, reaching out with his and hand to pull me up from the couch in one smooth motion.

"Treat me to coffee, which is the way into my heart," I joked, pulling myself from his grip to pick up my bag from a precarious pile of books, which spilled when I picked it up.

"My way and no one else's," he reminded me, as I nodded vaguely and made my way to his door.

"I have to go," I explained. "Duty calls."

"I'll see you after my date," He said. "Tinder duty calls."

I glared at him. He better be kidding. How was I going to introduce him to Regina if he was going to be late? He smiled, and I left his apartment without an idea if he was or he wasn't.

A couple of hours of utter chaos later, the event was finally starting. I was already dressed in my kooky Mrs. Peacock outfit—a flattering blue dress I had custom made in Kamuning once for only three hundred pesos (the seamstress charged me extra because it was, in her words, 'as big as a bed sheet') and my usual pair of comfortable work heels and one of Mags' favorite cat eye glasses. Sure my massive arms were exposed for all to see, but it was the only dress in my closet that suited the occasion.

"I can't believe you're not here," I said to Mags over the phone. "You ditched me for boys!"

"Calm down Ate, it's not a big deal!" Maggie promised. "And I told you, I don't like my guy friends that way."

I could hear her friends laughing and joking around in the background. They were hanging out at the mall not too far from this one, and despite Tita Merry's summon of the Aguas Clan, Maggie had bailed for the night. "We can watch *Clue* on YouTube or whatever."

"Yeah, but I thought you wanted to see Regina again, and see why everyone was invited, and dress up as Miss Scarlett," I pointed out. I knew I sounded a little petulant, but I couldn't help the feeling that I needed backup coming in to this thing, especially if I was going to face Regina again.

Meanwhile, I was running around with my head practically cut off trying to sort out the little emergencies that eventually come up during these sorts of events.

"Boo you, abandoner," I said to Maggie.

"It's because I have a social life," she answered back, and I rolled my eyes before she made kissing noises over the phone and hung up on me.

"Is my daughter being impossible?" Dad asked, coming up to me with Mom beside him. Since I'd been herding the event all afternoon, they had arrived with Benjo from the house after dropping Maggie off at the other mall. I sighed and shook my head.

"I think it depends which one we're talking about," Mom answered, squeezing my hand.

"Okay, okay, enough with you jokers, go out there and have some fun," I said, ushering them past the Boddy Mansion entrance. "And PS, you're late!"

"It's a Friday night on a payday weekend, sweetie, it is legit carmageddon out there," Mom said, and her impressive use of millennial lingo was always a little disturbing, so I ignored that and told them to make sure that they saw the kitchen since we constructed a passageway from the pantry to the living room, just like in the movie!

Mom and Dad wandered around the rooms, stopping by the exhibit we displayed of the Metropolitan Theatre in its current state, and the things they still needed to restore it. Apparently it was a great place to hang out in the seventies, so there were a lot of people their age in the crowd exchanging stories and talking about their escapades there.

I was in the registration booth, ushering guests inside and selling tickets. We were doing pretty well, but most of the guests asked me where Tita Merry was, and I honestly still had no idea. I had seen her once or twice in the course of the set-up, but had not really spoken to her once a small fiasco regarding the popcorn machine was settled. I hadn't eaten much that day, so I was munching on a bag of said popcorn while manning the booth, craving something sweet to go with it too.

I had seen some of the Aguas clan coming in by family to the event. Lola May, June, and April never left the house until one of them declared that they were going (all three of them were in their nineties now, and did everything together), and I wasn't surprised that they weren't here today. But I did see some of Lola June's children—second Titas and Titos already milling around, already saying hello to my parents. My aunts and uncles on Lola April's side of the family all lived in Alabang, an area of the south that hated making the drive to Manila without making a big fuss about the traffic. But there were a couple of Dad's cousins there. Some of them recognized me from reunions, others not really.

I hadn't seen Regina yet, which was the weird part. She promised she would be here with Tita Merry.

"One ticket please."

"Okay, may I have your...Enzo!" I exclaimed, not caring how wide my grin was when I saw him standing in front of the registration booth. He looked so cool in his Metropolitan Theatre shirt, which he classed up with a blazer. I recognized the logo from the NCCA's program of volunteer clean-ups for the theatre. He must have gone to one to get that shirt.

"Hey!" He said, equally surprised to see me sitting behind the registration desk. He went around the table as I stood up so he could kiss me cordially on the cheek. "This is a pleasant surprise. I heard there was a brilliant girl setting up this whole thing."

"It was no big deal," I shrugged, although I couldn't hide the blush on my cheeks.

"Oh it is," Enzo insisted, shaking his head and chuckling. "You have no idea. It's a relief, seeing you here, Martha."

We stepped away from the desk for a moment, edging towards a public but slightly more quiet spot on the side. He had his hand in his pocket, and the fingers of his other hand lightly on my elbow. Just that little touch made my body heat up and my throat tighten, like my muscles had memories of what we did together and longed to be used again. I cleared my throat to tamp down the feeling.

"How did you hear about the screening?" I asked him. He certainly wasn't on the invite list, even if the event was open to the public.

"I heard it from Tita Merry Benitez," he pointed out. "She...uh, well, she was persistent, to say the least. How do you know her?"

"Oh, she's my aunt," I said like it was no big deal. But the way Enzo reacted, I might as well have told him that I was the Queen of England. His eyes widened, and he gripped my elbow just a little tighter, like he needed to hold on to something.

As far as anchors went, I was a pretty good one.

See, I can make fat jokes!

"Er…are you okay?" I asked. He'd gone slightly pale, but recovered quickly by nodding. His hand disappeared just as quickly, and I tried very hard not to notice.

"Yeah," he said in a high pitched voice, before he coughed and recovered. "Yes. I just had no idea. So you're Regina's cousin?"

"Yeah!" I said a little too enthusiastically. "How did you—"

"Martha?" One of the event volunteers suddenly appeared next to us, holding a clipboard and wearing a nervous face. That did not bode well for me at all. Enzo and I blinked at her, and it made me wonder what we looked like, slightly tucked away and standing so close together that I could see where he cut himself shaving on his chin.

"They're just about ready for us to start seating in the theatre," she said. "But I can't seem to find the butler…"

We'd hired an actor to play the role of Tim Curry's Wadsworth to announce that the dinner party was about to begin in the theatre. Another one of Tita Merry's ideas, which I thought would add a nice touch to the evening. But apparently the actor she hired was a bit of a flake with a British accent.

"I'll look for him," I said, waving her off. "If he's not at his mark by 8:30, open the doors for everyone."

I threw Enzo an apologetic look and took off to look for out wayward actor. I felt slightly disappointed, leaving him in the middle of our conversation, but duty called. Where was Tita Merry?

* * *

"Oooh, ooh, this is my favorite part," I said to Max, tugging at his sleeve. We stood in the very back of the theatre, watching the full crowd watching the movie. Max walked in halfway through the film and stood next to me at the back where I could make sure everything was going smoothly. He hadn't seen *Clue* ever, so he was laughing through all of it with me.

My favorite part was when Missus White talked about her hate for Yvette (look it up, that scene is comedy gold), which I could repeat to Maggie when I described hate for certain people (Regina). I was pulling at Max's shirtsleeve through the whole thing, and by the end we were laughing so hard that people were glaring at us from their seats.

"Why is this the first time I am watching this?" Max asked, as we shared my large bucket of caramel popcorn.

"Because you and I haven't been friends long enough for my awesome to rub off on you," I joked, and we laughed again. My mind started to wander, and I vaguely looked around the theatre. I wondered where Enzo was sitting, who he was sitting with, when I realized that the movie was over and...

Was that Tita Merry coming to the front of the theatre? When did she get that microphone?

"Hello, hello everyone!" she said happily, and I could see most of my relatives waving back at her like they were greeting each other at the mall. She looked glorious, dressed in her own interpretation of Missus White, my favorite character in the movie. Tita Merry wore a wig and the same black dress as Madeline Kahn, complete with a string of pearls around her neck. "Did you enjoy the movie?"

The crowd cheered, clapping their hands.

"Well as you know, this was all to raise funds for a very important place to me and my husband Gerund..." she said, her voice trailing off slightly. Sometimes Tita Merry did that when she talked about Regina's dad, who I remembered as someone who was quite aloof and strict.

"We used to go to the Metropolitan Theatre every night we could to watch a show. So I dedicate my life to only two things now. The restoration of the theatre—"

More cheers from the crowd. Max and I even whooped to encourage her.

"And to make sure that my beautiful daughter Regina Marie is happy," she said, looking down at the spot where I assumed Regina was sitting. I hadn't seen her all night since I was busy with the event.

She looked just like she did when we were kids—tall, thin, demure and delicately beautiful. Though we were related, we looked nothing alike.

"With that said, I think you have something to say to her, Lorenzo?" Tita Merry asked, bringing me back into the room as I saw Enzo stand up from his seat next to Regina and smile nervously before he stepped up to the center of the room.

Behind him, a photo presentation started to flash of Regina walking past a London phone booth, laughing at someone behind the camera, mouthing words that we couldn't hear. Then there was Regina pouting at the cameraman offering her an egg tart before she bit it off his fingers. Regina toasting him, looking beautiful in the dim lighting of a bar.

"Hello," Enzo said into the microphone, and I felt my heart shattering into a thousand tiny pieces. It all made sense suddenly. His nerves, Regina's insistence that I be there tonight, Tita Merry's disappearance… Enzo wasn't just here for the Met. "My name is Enzo, and I met Regina for the first time in London…"

His words melted away as the evidence of what I had missed nearly blinded me. I wasn't even conscious that I was stuffing my face with caramel popcorn until Max stopped my hand midway to my mouth and gave me an odd look.

"What?" I asked him with my cheeks full of sweet, painful bitterness. I wanted to leave, and I knew that I should. But you know when you're on the road and you see an accident, and you just can't look away? That's what that moment felt like. There was nothing else for me to do but fill my mouth with sugar and popcorn.

"Regina, will you marry me?"

The roar of the crowd's cheering drowned out her answer, but the kiss they shared was unmistakable. Tita Merry was wiping her eyes with the handkerchief Dad passed to her as they watched Regina and her new fiancé Enzo smile at the crowd of well-wishers.

"I think I need to throw up," I said, pushing Max aside to go to the bathroom.

"This isn't healthy, you know," Max said, standing outside the closed stall while I stood inside, held my breath, and swallowed air to throw up or pass out. Either one would be preferable at the moment. I glared at the toilet, picturing the sheer amount of food that I'd consumed in the last twelve hours. Popcorn, fast food, a burrito, cookies…come on, come on! I need to get this awful, sickening feeling out of my stomach.

I gagged on air. I could feel something starting to rise up from my stomach. Here it comes, here it comes…

"Can you please get out of there?" Max asked, so close to the door that I saw his shoes peeping inside. "You're scaring the shit out of me, Martha."

Suddenly the desire to gag vanished as quickly as it had come, and I took a step back from the toilet. Max was uncomfortable, and I was making him uncomfortable with what I was doing. I closed my eyes and took a couple of deep breaths. This wasn't me at all! I don't do this, and I certainly wasn't going to start now.

Willpower, Martha. That's all you need.

I emerged from the stall to find Max leaning against the frame, his glare severe. He had apparently locked the door to the women's bathroom, and I could hear people trying to get in. We were alone.

"Mind explaining what that was?" he asked, nudging his head towards the stall. He sounded like Dad when I did something wrong, and I hated it immediately.

"None of your business, that's what," I said, walking to the sinks. I couldn't bear to look at myself, so I glared at my hands as I needlessly washed them, letting the water just run over my fingers. Max sauntered over to the sink next to me.

"That wasn't nothing," he said sternly. "Martha, you were about to make yourself throw up! And why, because someone you liked got engaged to your cousin?"

Something inside me twisted, reminding me that the awful feeling I had was still inside, and looking for a way to get out. I grabbed the soap and put some into my hands. Then I started talking before I could stop myself.

"You don't get it," I snapped at him, so suddenly and so fast that I didn't even realize that I was doing it. I kept my eyes down and my hands under the water. "Enzo wasn't just this boy that I liked in college, Max! I was in love with him! Enzo is, was the first…the first real boy I've ever fallen in love with."

"You don't know what it's like to spend four years watching someone from a distance, never feeling that you were good enough for him because you wear pants that could fit around him twice! You don't know how strange, and, and wonderful and new it felt to me when he knew my name, when he called me or laughed at something that I said."

"You will never, ever understand how much it hurts that in the end, he still chose someone as beautiful and perfect as Regina. Because of course the fat girl doesn't get the boy. That's not nothing, Max! That is everything, everything…"

He reached over and turned off the faucet. I looked down at my ugly, wrinkled hands and clenched them. If I was crying, big, ugly, fat tears, I didn't notice or care right now.

He was so close I could pick out the individual threads on the buttons of his shirt. So close that I could see his chest rising and falling.

"Don't cry, okay?" he said, and I couldn't. My heart was hammering in my ears and my lungs were screaming for breath. He placed a hand on my shoulder. "Martha…"

"I don't want your pity, Max." I said, pushing him away. There was a pause, and I didn't have the heart to see the way he looked at me. This was the first time I'd broken down in front of him, and it reminded both of us how new and fragile this friendship of ours was. I wiped the tears from my eyes, rubbing it hard.

"Okay," he said, stepping back. "Okay."

Suddenly my friend was back, and acting like nothing had ever happened. I watched him adjust his sleeves in the mirror, ruffle his hair slightly, slightly confused. Was this how Max dealt with things? Just pushed them aside and act like they didn't happen?

He took a piece of tissue from the counter and passed it to me. My breathing started to even out, and running the tissue under cold water helped lower the swelling of my eyes.

"So what are you going to do?" he asked me. "Get a sexy, revenge body before the wedding?"

"Yeah right, I like I could give up chocolate that easily," I snorted.

"I have no doubt that you can," he shrugged. "Do it for the right reasons, though."

Then we were quiet for a few moments. Me, finally finding the courage to look at myself straight in the mirror again, and Max making stupid faces and posing in front of the mirror. I know he was trying to distract me from my feelings. He was trying to make me laugh.

"Max Angeles," he said in a fake American accent. "You are a sexy man. Smokin' even. All the girls drop their trousers—"

"What the heck…"

"Just to grab your attention. Tell us! What did you do to be blessed with such a handsome face?" he said to the mirror.

"Oh just the proper diet, exercise and the love of a good woman is all a hunk needs," He said as I finally smiled and rolled my eyes. He grinned at me. "Now there's the Martha I know. Are we going back out there or are we bailing?"

I quickly checked my phone. Three missed calls from Regina, one from Tita Merry and one from Mom. I sighed and showed them to him quickly.

"Duty calls," I said, tossing the tissues into the trash bin. Max shrugged and walked to the door when I realized where we were. He'd just locked the door to the women's bathroom. Anyone who would see us walk out would think we were…

"Dude!"

"What?" He asked, his hand already halfway to the door handle. He looked genuinely surprised. Then I remembered that this wasn't the first time we were in a bathroom together.

Then I looked down at myself, at my large arms, blotchy face and slightly matted hair. Right. Like anyone would think we had sex in the bathroom! I smiled and shook my head.

"Nothing," I said, walking over to him to open the door myself. "Thank you. For this."

"Anytime, Martha," he said. "Oh, and one last thing. Indulge me."

"Okay?"

"You're much stronger than you think," he said, "Believe in that."

He gave me a wink and a quick kiss on the cheek before walking back out to the party with me. I stopped in shock, my hand immediately flying to the spot where his lips had been. My face felt hot, and if I was worried that we looked like we had sex in a public bathroom, this wasn't helping any.

Not that this meant anything, of course. Max was just being nice. But I couldn't deny it was just what I needed. Some of the women waiting outside the door gasped at the sight of us and looked me up from head to toe. I could see a couple of them focusing on my flabby arms. I shrugged and smiled at them before following Max back to the mansion set-up.

* * *

The bi-monthly Aguas Family Sunday brunch was always, always held at my grandmother, Lola May's house in Antipolo. It was a small but elegant house with three bedrooms and a den that she maintained with a small staff of four—a driver, a house girl, a full-time nurse, and a part-time cook. Dad, Tita Merry, and their other sisters always asked Lola May to live with them, with her being ninety and all, but she always insisted on living on her own. There was no reason for her not to, she said.

I loved Lola May. At seventy six, her mind was incredibly sharp, she loved playing sudoku and beating her cook, driver, and nurse in mahjong every week. Her house was tucked away in the wilder parts of Antipolo and had a fantastic view of the entire city below. We usually ate in the dining room, had merienda in the garden of wildflowers in her backyard, which was surrounded by calamansi trees. Regina used to climb up those trees and put my dolls there, knowing I would be too scared to go up.

There was no Wi-Fi, and very rarely did we have phone signal (Lola still used her landline to call her children). It was a place out of time, and I loved it.

I found Regina in the garden that afternoon, sitting under the biggest calamansi tree with her eyes closed and her hands over her lap. Her engagement ring sparkled in the noontime sun, and she looked like she was soaking every bit of sunshine that bathed her. She inherited the signature Aguas wavy hair and thin lips, but her aquiline nose and slightly darker skin was a Benitez trait. Lola May used to call her the 'little beauty queen' of the family.

We didn't exactly get along, and I couldn't help that little stab of jealousy I always felt when I saw her in her favorite little shift dresses with her long legs splayed out in front of her. The engagement ring only made the jealousy worse.

"Psst!" I called out to her, interrupting her downtime under the tree. "Didn't Lola May tell you the trees were infested with fire ants?"

That made her eyes pop open before she jumped up and checked her bright yellow sundress, her back, her arms and the tree. I was clutching my sides by the time she caught on and gave me a little glare.

"I can't believe I fell for that!" she exclaimed.

I shrugged, ready to turn back to the house. To my utter surprise, Regina came over and hugged me so tightly that I thought she was trying to lift me off the ground. What on earth? Regina and I never hugged. We weren't friends! We just happened to share a middle and last name.

"Uh…" I said awkwardly. "Okay."

"Sorry, I couldn't help it," she said. "I missed you!"

Oh did she? Missed someone to torture, more like.

"So, er, how long are you going to grace us with your presence this time?" I asked, pulling away from the hug.

"How about…forever?" Regina asked. "I took an indefinite leave of absence from school."

"Huh?" I asked. "Why?"

Her answer fell on deaf ears when Mags came running up to Regina to give her a hug. Regina just turned into the sweetest person in the world when it came to Maggie, like she was actually her baby sister. She and Maggie were now squealing at each other, exclaiming how thin Maggie was, how fantastic Regina looked.

"I'm down to a large now, can you believe it?" Maggie asked, and I saw a twinkle of excitement in her eyes. I felt a twinge of pride with the little green monster of jealousy taking over my throat. I was happy that Maggie was losing weight. She worked hard for it, and she seemed to like the process. But was I jealous?

Only very little, in a way that you felt jealous when a classmate had that Backstreet Boys cassette tape you've been saving up for.

Maggie and Regina's talking started from the garden and went on all the way to the actual merienda. For some reason, Regina knew most of the friends of Maggie's friends (or something) and they were lost in gossip for most of the afternoon.

We hadn't even gotten around to really talking about the engagement until merienda in the garden. Mid-afternoon meals were all about gossip with a cup of hot chocolate and tea, especially in my grandmother's house.

We were served a wide array of treats. Lola enjoyed feeding her family with homemade purple yam jam (her secret recipe), delicate rolls of sweet milk treats, called pastillas from Lukban, small round discs of *bibingka* rice cake and cheesy, translucent *pichi-pichi* snacks from one of her friends.

Drinks were always the same, barako coffee for the adults (extra strong for Papa) and tablea hot chocolate for the grandchildren. If there was anything Lola loved to do more than play a round of Chinese mahjong, it was feeding her family.

The engagement was understandably buried under Regina's stories from London and our exclamations over the food. Maggie announced she had decided to go into Fine Arts for college, which sparked a discussion about an old friend of Tita Merry's that was the friend of the former dean, who happened to also know someone who knew someone...

We were in the middle of talking about a second cousin of ours who migrated to the US with her boyfriend who was ten years older than her when Enzo walked into the garden. He treated every room like a stage, his role perfectly clear to him. He dutifully smiled and lightly placed his forehead under the adults' extended fingers for mano, he politely called my dad 'Tito' and my grandmother Lola. He kissed Maggie on the cheek like they'd known each other forever. He looked at Regina like she was his entire world, and me like an afterthought.

"I had no idea Reg was your cousin," he said to me, bussing my cheek. I felt it burn and smolder, curls of smoke disappearing against my cheek as I forced the feeling away. "You have no idea how nice it is to have a friendly face around."

"I'm not exactly a friendly face," I wanted to say, but stopped myself as Enzo settled in on a seat beside Regina. She smiled and pat his leg.

"You've met Martha?" Regina asked.

"You could say that," I said, raising a skeptical eyebrow at Enzo. Did he not tell her about us?

They looked good together, and fit together. Seeing them made sense, and the engagement ring on Regina's finger was icing on the cake. How could I go against that?

It was only until Tita Merry put down her cup of coffee that the discussion began. I was in the middle of refusing another round of pichi-pichi, which made Regina widen her eyes.

"What do you mean, you don't want Tita Chi's *pichi-pichi*?" she asked suspiciously. "They're your favorite! Are you on a diet or something?"

I hated major assumption number one, that just because I didn't want to eat, I was automatically on a diet. It was a Filipino thing I guess. Any young lady of a certain age was always eating too much ('*hija*, you really should go on a diet!') or eating too little ('ay hija, are you on a diet? Eat more!'). I know Regina didn't mean anything by her comment, but it still stung.

"Oh please, me? On a diet?" I scoffed. "I really..."

Tita Merry called everyone inside by ringing a small silver bell Lola May purchased from Florence once. We all went inside as she stood at the head of the table like a CEO.

"As you all know," she said like she was leading a power brunch instead of a family affair. "And I've already given Mama the full story, Regina recently got engaged to Lorenzo."

I snorted while sipping my tsokolate, as did Maggie. Of course Tita Merry used Enzo's full name to address him. I shouldn't be surprised. According to the play-by-play she mentioned over lunch, Enzo had approached her to help coordinate his proposal at the screening, which explained why she was forever absent during the event itself. Apparently this engagement was a year in the making too.

But to everyone else outside the Aguas-Benitez circle, this whole thing was nothing short of a surprise. Maggie usually talked to Regina over Facebook, and there was no mention of Enzo then. When they Skyped once, there was a mention of a boyfriend, but nothing too serious. Mom simply reminded us that Tita Merry had her own life, and Regina did too. Our job was to just be happy for them and help them when they asked for it.

That was the thing about families, wasn't it? You were consulted, asked for help, and you never agreed with half the things they did, but you loved them anyway.

Talk about complicated.

"So we're quite ready to proceed with the plans," Tita Merry continued, brandishing a previously unseen baby pink trapper keeper (yes the kind you used to have in Grade School) from her seat. I saw Regina sigh a little at the sight of it. I saw Dad jump when Tita Merry slapped the gigantic 1990s trapper keeper on to the table.

"Ever since she turned eighteen, I have been booking Regina for a wedding at Magallanes church," she promptly informed the table, which made Reg's eyes widen. That was apparently news to her. "I make that reservation year after year. Mellie the church's secretary is always on my Christmas gift list. You remember last year, when I gave Mellie the *quezo de bola* spread, Charity?"

My mother, who to everyone else in the universe was Chari, barely looked up from her plate of bibingka when she nodded. I could tell by the shake of her shoulders she was laughing, whether at being called Charity or the special Edam cheese spread, I would never know. My Dad was squeezing her arm, trying to get her giggles to stop. Tita Merry didn't see it, but cleared her throat.

"So the wedding will be in December this year, so we don't have much time."

"Why the rush?" my mother asked curiously. "Are you preggy, Regina?"

"Regina Marie!" my grandmother exclaimed, slapping her hand on the table. She was a Luz, a family with alta sociedad Spanish and Batangueño roots. She was very traditional. In her mind, proper ladies didn't drink wine until they were 21, and children were strict second class citizens in a family gathering. Until we turned eighteen, we were made to eat in the kitchen rather than the main dining room.

Major assumption number two: any woman marrying early or quickly must be pregnant already. Regina laughed it off while Enzo choked lightly on his food. I was only too happy to thump his back for him until it cleared out.

"No, Lola!" Regina exclaimed, shaking her head just to emphasize her point. "Promise! I just want to do it quickly, that's all."

"And anyway, Lorenzo's parents and I have already agreed on the date," Tita Merry exclaimed. I saw Regina turn to Enzo for confirmation and he nodded. "It's the best date since we have my sisters coming in very soon. Your Titas Flora and Fauna booked their tickets back to Manila last night."

"Yes, did they say why they booked so suddenly?" Lola May asked. "Those tickets must have been expensive."

"Yeah, and we all know Ate Flora only likes riding first class," Dad pointing out, sipping his coffee. "She usually doesn't book a ticket until it's at least half-off."

"I have no idea why they decided to fly in so fast, but they are arriving next week so they can be part of the every-all!" Tita Merry exclaimed. We would soon find out that she had this uncanny ability to spin every topic we discussed to steer towards the wedding. The weather today was warm? That's why she booked December so the wedding would be cool. Global warming? Surely not before the wedding!

By every-all, she meant the general festivities that came with a wedding. And here in the Philippines, that meant a lot. There was the traditional *pamamanhikan*, the engagement party, bridal showers, reunions if relatives were coming in…the list was potentially endless. Since the happy couple was getting married in a year, more or less, that didn't give us much time.

Did I say us? I meant them. They didn't have much time.

"So, we have the pamamanhikan and engagement celebration in exactly a month with both families and a large party," Tita Merry announced, consulting her calendar. This hyper-organized Tita was completely new to me. Usually Tita Merry was a bit scatterbrained—I had to remind her of certain things when I organized events for her, and she always worried she forgot to do something. But with this, she seemed totally confident in herself, and ready to take this whole thing on. "Enzo's family has graciously allowed us to host them—"

"Which sounds very odd to me," Lola May pointed out, tutting her disappointment. We all knew that traditionally, the groom's family invited the bride's family to their home so the son may formally ask the bride's parents for their daughter's hand in marriage.

But Tita Merry wanted to do away with that tradition (not doing it with Tito Gerund made her too sad, Regina explained later) and simply have a big engagement party with the asking as a part of the program. Not exactly the most traditional of pamamanhikans.

"Now Martha, as the Matron-of-Honor, may I entrust you with this?"

Now it was my turn to choke on my food. I heard Maggie hoot with laughter and I wanted to drop kick her. Enzo was only too happy to return the favor I did for him and thumped on my back, which made me glare slightly at him while he sheepishly smiled. Regina shook her head.

"Mamá!" she exclaimed. "She's still single, so it's Maid-of honor."

"Loool Ate's a matron!" Maggie exclaimed from her seat, and I glared daggers at her to get her to stop. Lola May shook her head at me like she found me hilarious.

"And I haven't even asked her yet!" Regina exclaimed, immediately reaching over Enzo's front to reach for my hand. She ended up half-sprawled over him since my arms were not that long. "I'm so sorry Marths, I was going to do this whole thing with a necklace and a card for you…"

Me? Her Maid-of-Honor? Over my dead body. Over my dog's dead body (sorry, Bibi). No way. No freaking way.

"It's no big deal," I said, turning to her to give her a tight smile, which Enzo actually returned, and I looked away sharply.

I shouldn't be bothered by this. Enzo and I were just friends now. I had no claims over him except that one night, that one night that I had kept so close to myself. I thought I would never see him again, that I would keep the memory just as it was…secret and all mine. Now here he was, real as can be, but he was Regina's now. My brain couldn't process it. I needed a little time.

Telling Regina about the past was Enzo's job…right?

"Perfect!" Tita Merry said, jotting something down. "So Martha is organizing the pamamanhikan. This is going to be a big deal, my dear. The Benitezes are expecting a big to-do, since Regina here is the oldest grandchild. We'll make sure to put their money where our mouths are."

I felt the color drain from my face and my hands go slightly clammy as my father corrected Tita Merry. Planning events for her charities was okay, but an engagement party with Tita Flora, Fauna and Merryweather Aguas breathing down my neck? Did she think I was agreeing to it?

I didn't have the emotional strength to handle any of this. I was barely holding it together.

"No, Tita, I—" I began. Tell her you have a full time job! And a dog!

"Thank you for volunteering, hija, it's going to be a huge help to me and Regina," Tita Merry said, smiling and tapping my hand affectionately as my jaw dropped to the table. I wanted to scream and tell everyone that I couldn't go through with this. I wanted to storm off and just leave bloody Antipolo so I didn't have to do any of this.

Instead I deflated slightly and grabbed a piece of pichi-pichi.

* * *

"I don't think we're going to get along," I said, sliding Max's phone to his side of the table and glaring at him a week later. We were sitting in his favorite restaurant, a kebab place he went to so often that the staff knew his name. I had to admit, the shawarma rice was pretty fantastic.

We were eating out because Max was consulting with me over his accounting and other business practices. He was the most dedicated vet I knew (although I admit I didn't know a lot), and he really enjoyed running the clinic, but he was admittedly too scatterbrained to handle the administrative work himself. So our office helped him out, and he was more than happy to have us on retainer.

I was helping him make sense of his finances while he sorted out his patient files and told me about his regular patients, his favorites, recounting the giraffe birth for the fourth time (I loved hearing that story because Max got hit in the forehead by the calf's hoof and passed out).

One of the older waitresses had come over to comment how nice it was that Max "finally found me" as she gave me another serving of rice. I was too high on the amazing garlic sauce to really care, and continued to eat with gusto. That was, until Max announced he was seeing someone.

"Ha-ha, nice try, liar," I said, squeezing more garlic sauce over my plate.

"I'm not kidding," he insisted, pulling his phone out from underneath his

57

clinic files to show me the photo.

Her name was Georgina Torres, or George for short. She brought her little Bichon Frisé to his clinic for anti-rabies shots one day, and according to Max, she was "so gorgeous it would have been a crime not to flirt with her." I was a bit dubious about this until I looked her up on Facebook (it didn't take long since she'd taken to tagging Max in every possible post) where she posted a selfie of herself and Max with the caption, "walking the babies with my bae."

Like, calm down girl, it's only been two days. Max has had relationships with cake slices longer than with you.

"She's…" I frowned, wondering what I would say to put it delicately. "I don't know. There's something unlikeable about her."

"What are you talking about, the photo already has five hundred likes," he pointed out, peering down at the photo again. It was a nice photo, optimal lighting, a nice filter and a big smile from her. Max, I wasn't too convinced about yet. He didn't get selfies, why people needed to constantly take pictures of themselves. When he posted, it was always a photo of the book he was reading, or of Wookie, a candid photo of me once in a while.

And suddenly he was converted to the power of a selfie? I don't think so.

"She has a Bichon, Max! Never trust a girl with a Bichon Frisé, their owners tend to be more high maintenance than them," I warned him.

"Is that a piece of wisdom you picked up from an Internet video?" Max said quickly, and I narrowed my eyes at him. Now I knew something was off. Since when did he watch Internet videos? Since when was he so defensive about a girl he was dating? He never usually told me more about them than their name. What was so different about this one? Did he forget that he was the one who told me about the Bichon Bitch?

He must have noticed the beginnings of my annoyance bubbling up from inside so he dropped his steady gaze.

"Look," he sighed. "Just…be nice if I introduce you, okay? She already feels threatened by you as it is…"

I put on a scandalized face, dropping my jaw, and bugging out my eyes. Max gave me the same narrow-eyed look I'd just thrown at him, and I shrugged it off.

"What?" I asked innocently. "I just find it hard to believe a bae with a 'banging body' like hers would be threatened by the girl who could break her in half by sitting on her."

It was a joke we both knew didn't land. Max never enjoyed it when I self-deprecated. We both frowned and looked down at our food. Clearly this wasn't a good day for either of us.

I mashed my rice and garlic sauce together on my plate, contemplating ordering a lassi yogurt while I slowly processed what Max was trying to do. I couldn't imagine him going out with someone. Maybe I hadn't known him for long enough, or maybe I'd never seen him show such a keen interest in anyone else. And why should I not be happy for him? He was handsome, a dog-lover, with a business of his own, and he was so well-read I couldn't catch up with him. Sure he was a little scatterbrained at times, but that was what I was for, right?

"Okay, I'm sorry," I said so quickly he wouldn't have heard it if he wasn't listening out for it. I reached across the table and squeezed his hand. His elbow was resting over a copy of *Love in the Time of Cholera*, which should have tipped me off about his current mental state. Why was he so determined that I know about this girl? He's never talked about his other dates before, much less plan to introduce them to me.

I pretended to review his papers to put us back on the topic of the clinic. But I couldn't.

"I'll be nice," I promised. "I'll smile and compliment her and make her feel pretty."

"That's not..." Max said, taking a deep breath to calm himself down before he talked again. "That's not what I want, and you know that."

So what did he want? I wanted this kind energy to dissipate, I wanted to talk to him about this Enzo thing. But with that look of his face, I knew it was the last thing he wanted to do.

"I have to go," I said, fishing my wallet out of my bag to pay for my half of dinner before I started gathering up the files I would need to review later. "I have to..."

"Yeah," was all he said, raising his hand to ask for the bill. Tito Bob of Tito Bob's Shawarma House came over and made a whole fuss about how I shouldn't pay when I was the one being taken out to lunch. Tito Bob was a very large, very gay man who used to work in Turkey as a dishwasher in a famous Turkish shish-kabob place.

After three years, he got fed up, asked his boss point blank just what made his shawarma so good and came home to open his own place. He'd known Max since he moved to Manila from Los Baños, and claimed he was the one who put the lean in Max's figure. Char!

"Ay, Tito Bob, we're not—"

I began to protest, but he squeezed my hand and shook his head vehemently before he waggled his fingers at Max.

"Hoy, Max! I don't give you the best table in my restaurant so you can be ungentlemanly to your *uber-ganders* girl!" he scolded Max, swatting him lightly with the fluorescent yellow fly swatter he always had about his person. "You already brought her to the cheapest place in town, the least you can do is pay!"

No amount of explanation on my part would deter Tito Bob's surprisingly traditional beliefs about my relationship with Max ('I have never heard of a girl being expected to pay for her meal when she's on a date!'). Max sighed and placed the bills on the table, gathered up the files, his book, and nodded his head toward the door. I was too distracted by Tito Bob asking about Max's kissing technique ('I bet he's sloppy but really tender, *charot*!') to be surprised that Max was holding my hand as we walked out.

It was only when Tito Bob looked down at our linked hands and gave me a knowing look that I realized we were doing it.

Oh. We were holding hands.

We stood outside together, our hands still clasped together. I know it should be a big deal to someone, but it wasn't, right? No big deal. Friends held hands all the time, didn't they?

But he couldn't look me in the eye for some reason. Maybe he was still mad about what I said about Georgia. Or was he? I hated not knowing.

My hands were starting to get clammy, so I made the excuse of fishing out money from my wallet to pay for my half of lunch. Max frowned and leaned over, placing a hand on the small of my back before whispering, "Tito Bob's watching."

Lo and behold, he was. Tito Bob watched us from the restaurant door, and he was actually gathering his wait staff and pointing at us specifically. I realized that this was the first time in two years that anyone had ever assumed that Max and I were a couple. It was a strange feeling, and I knew I would have found this hilarious if he wasn't in such a bad mood. Maybe he would find it funny later.

"Where are you off to?" he asked, leading me gently to his car. "I'll drop you off on my way to meet George. We're taking the dogs to that fancy place in Taguig for a jog."

There were a lot of jokes I could make about pretty, cropped-shirt wearing Georgia Torres jogging dogs with slobby, rough, leave-me-alone-to-read Max, but decided it was prudent to just hold my tongue.

"I'm meeting Reg then we're picking up our aunts at the airport," I said. "I can get a car or something."

"Martha..."

"Max," I said, turning to him with a bright, confident smile on my face. "It's okay."

I had this odd feeling that I was talking about something other than our transportation arrangements. But I smiled and ignored that feeling. Max gave me a solemn nod, like he knew it too. My phone beeped with a text message.

> Regina: Is it just me or has Taguig gotten fancier than the last time I was here? Anyway, here at Fully Booked. Are you excited for the Three Witches to reunite??? because I'm not

> Martha: Something wicked this way comes, and I am not looking forward to it either. Taking an Uber. See you there!

> Regina: xx

> Martha: What is that?

Regina: Oh, sorry! Its kisses. British thing. Don't worry about it.

Shortly after Regina asked me to be her Maid-of-Honor, Maggie quickly pulled me aside to tell me that Regina…had changed. Apparently she was determined to become my friend, and that I should try too.

I told Maggie that I wasn't the one who dressed up in a big, sparkly ballgown at my own seventh birthday, but promised to make an effort. So Regina and I were texting all chummy-like. I had to admit, if I didn't know about her little evil ways as a child, we would make really good buddies.

Did this mean she was already growing on me?

Martha: Okay. Have to talk to you about something, by the way. About Enzo.

MESSAGE SENDING FAILED

Six

TRAFFIC. TRAFFIC EVERYWHERE.

Regina was practically bouncing off the walls of our van as we rushed headlong into the traffic-lined streets. The entire four lanes of C-5 was crammed to the gills with private cars making their way to the expressway, and we were stuck there until we reached the small service road heading to the direction of the airport.

Kuya Benjo was muttering curses under his breath as he navigated the road, and not for the first time, I was glad that I wasn't the one driving. Tita Merry was in the front captain's chair, dead asleep. She hated sitting in vans as much as Regina, but always took the more passive approach and simply fell asleep behind a pair of cat eye sunglasses. I could swear I heard snoring. Our van was the only car big enough to fit us, the titas and their luggage, since, they announced they were bringing home two boxes each.

Meanwhile, Regina was playing EDM out loud from her phone and getting antsy. She was almost squirming in her seat, trying to get comfortable for longer than a minute. I've known my cousin long enough to know that she hated being confined in small spaces for any more than an hour. She was impossible to bring along on road trips that way.

"AAAAAH," she exclaimed, as we moved another inch forward. The car jerked a little and I felt my entire body jiggle at the movement. I crossed my arms over my chest and frowned.

Oh my god my bra was utterly useless! Whatever size I bought, my boobs always ended up spilling over the top and jiggling with every step I took. A classmate of mine once told this horror story of a woman with such large boobs that she needed to lift one every time she showered when her breasts sagged. It was a story that haunted me sometimes.

There was nothing great about having large breasts. They're heavy, clunky, and very hard to wear tops with. Girls with smaller chests always tell me how jealous they were of my 'assets' because guys loved big boobs, but the guy I wanted would like me in spite of my massive boobs. My boobs have been made fun of, popped out, and sucked in. I wouldn't trade them for anything but...could they be just a little more discreet?

"I take it your digital marketing workshop was a success." I said to my phone, leaning against the car window. Technically I was on an extended lunch break from work, but was always on call for the clients to contact me. It was a part of the job.

Right then I was talking to Mindy who had taken a digital marketing seminar. The company gave a small allowance allocation for technical learning, and Mindy took this after she heard it was for the hip, the cool, and the fabulous. "Did they wow you with their super hip, Gen Z insights?"

"Oh boy did they...not," Mindy said, and I could feel her sarcasm from a few miles away. "Here's hoping Whitney Houston was wrong, because if these children are our future then we are screwed."

I chuckled. I knew Mindy was a little miffed that I didn't go with her, but there was nobody else available to coordinate with Kuya Benj to pick up the Titas from the airport. Mindy and I continued to discuss the workshop, and I helped relay what the client wanted to achieve with their marketing push.

"By the way, did we send those filing notices for the Eastwick people?" Mindy asked, and I could hear her nervously tapping her pen on the desk. Between that and Regina's music, I could barely hear a thing.

"Yes, and I've already filed the billing requests," I said a little loudly. Thankfully Regina got the hint and lowered the volume on her phone. "I'm dropping by the office later, we can talk about the workshop."

"Gotcha boss! See you later." Mindy exclaimed. "By the way, are you dating that Max guy? I remember you talk to him on the phone a lot, so I stalked him a little on Facebook, and dang girl, he is hawt!"

"Okay, bye Mindy!" I chirped and hung up just in time to notice that Regina was looking at me with a fond little smile.

"Yes?" I asked her curiously, putting away my phone.

"Look at you saying things like 'billing' and 'workshop'," she said, patting my thigh lightly (it still jiggled). "You're a full grown up now, girl."

"Thanks," I said, raising my eyebrow as I put away my phone. "But you're way more grown up than me. Tita Merry mentioned you were a semester away from graduating."

Something about that made Regina crumble and shut off almost immediately, her hand retreating back to her lap. God, what was with today? Everything I said set people off so easily.

"Yeah, I don't see myself coming back for that," Regina finally said nonchalantly. "Enzo's got a pretty good job here, and Mama's talking about setting up a foundation for her charity work…this is my home now, you know? Traffic and all," she said, looking out at the crowded road as we inched forward. She was staring at nothing so intently that I could almost see the wheels in her head turning.

If you looked Regina up on Instagram (her medium of choice), you could tell that there was a lot of curation that came in to it. All her posts were pretty and polished, the kind that took her hours to filter and caption, showing off her silly streak with the gorgeous buildings of London in the background. She was always happy and completely content, and there was no trace of a desire to leave.

Apparently, the Internet was an illusion, and now was the only time I only saw what was really going on behind the lovely filters and Regina's punny captions. Her 3,000 follower strong account took time, planning, and plotting which of her artworks to post, when peak hours were and what to hash tag. She liked to joke that it was one of the few times her art management degree came in handy.

Looking at her now, biting her nail worriedly and her foot tapping incessantly against the car interiors, I caught a glimpse of the little girl I grew up with, the one who forced me to get over my need for a night light by holding my hand in one of our many sleepovers. In a weird way, Regina was right. She'd finally come home.

But why leave London in the first place?

"Listen, Regina," I said, shaking my head. As her cousin and someone who just wanted her to be happy, I needed to tell her about Enzo, ask her what happened. She seemed just a little lost. "We need to talk."

But just as she was about to open her mouth to agree, our car made it to the service lane, and my phone started ringing. It was a client whose call I had been waiting for, and kept me occupied all the way to the airport, where I was gesturing madly at Kuya Benjo to the titas, who I could already see.

Tita Merry woke up as soon as we got to the airport. I wasn't surprised that we were able to spot Tita Flora and her twin sister Tita Fauna waiting for us from three bays away.

Tita Flora was, as always, wearing the biggest hat within a five-meter radius. Her brightly-patterned floral dress blew lightly in the warm summer wind as she raised her perfectly manicured hand to flag us down. Beside her was Tita Fauna, the very picture of propriety in her patterned shift dress and rubber sole flats, very practical, and in her signature shade of navy blue.

They were twin sisters, the oldest of the Aguas family. When Tita Flora retired seven years ago from her practice in Virginia, her twin made good on a childhood promise they made to spend the last of their days at a beach house in Malibu, where they both lived now.

Between them, they had one child (our cousin Lydia, who still lived in Virginia with her perfect husband and super-cute son) and three cats. Tita Flora's ex-husband was a Greek billionaire that had eschewed a prenup, and she made out with half of his money after she found him in bed with two other women. Tita Merry rounded out their little band of the Three Witches, a name my father frequently called them to their faces.

"Oh dear, look at you Martha!" Tita Flora exclaimed as I came over to greet her with the usual mano and kiss on the cheek. "Hija, you look so... hmmm...healthy!"

Strike one from Tita Flora. At the corner of my eye, I saw Tita Fauna twitch, and I knew she was about to follow up with a hit.

"Yes, yes, I saw your posts on the Facebook for your trip to Korea! You must have eaten a lot, your cheeks are quite puffy, dear. But you were alone? So scary!" she said, pouting her lips to the right side of her face to exaggerate the soft skin on her cheek, which I politely bushed with my own cheek. "I can't believe Philip and Chari let you go like that. You should at least have a boy with you to ward off predators."

I saw Tita Merry's ears perk up and knew I was in for the full experience of the wrath of my titas. I braced myself for the comment, but before I could, Regina literally leapt in front of her mother to interrupt her.

"Okay, let's go to the car and go home!" Regina exclaimed, saving me from the scrutiny of my aunts. I gave her a tiny smile in gratitude as we all piled back in to the van, both of us squeezing together with their luggage in the back while the Aunties got a row each to themselves. Tita Flora began fanning herself with her giant hat while asking Benj to turn the AC up.

The car jumped when we hit a speed bump, and all three of them went, 'ay ee-nang!', which had them laughing at their own silliness.

I had to admit, I missed seeing the three of them together. They loved making each other laugh, and telling us embarrassing stories about my dad's childhood, like that time when he grew lettuce in the garden thinking it was weed. Some days, Maggie and I couldn't wait to be titas like them.

Some days though, we were glad we weren't there yet.

What was Tita Flora's big announcement, though? Knowing her, she was waiting for the whole family to be together before she would say anything. I studied her, wondering what she could possibly say that she needed to be back home for. Was she getting married again?

"...so we're having the party on the fifteenth, then it's all the way to the wedding in December," Tita Merry was saying. "Regina and Martha are planning the engagement party. They promise it's going to be a big event."

"Good, because I would imagine the Benitezes would not be happy if it was small, god forbid," Tita Fauna said, rolling her eyes. She turned to us. "Just tell us if you need advice, girls."

"How about you just tell us about your fiancée instead, Regina?" Tita Flora asked, reaching behind her to wave her bejeweled fingers at Regina until she awkwardly took Tita's hand and shook with her. Regina and I exchange amused looks. "Come on, tell us how you met, and the proposal!"

For some reason this made Regina uncomfortable, and she started fiddling with her engagement ring. I decided it was a good time as any to return the favor and save her from the aunts' scrutiny. But this was getting seriously odd.

"Tita, it was so magical, they got engaged at the mansion scene Tita Merry and I set up for a screening," I said, my brain scrambled for something to tell them, something that would throw their focus off completely. "My friend Max said it gave him butterflies of *kilig*."

Oh shit. I realized quickly that I just made the worst possible error. I mentioned the one thing I knew I shouldn't even mention when talking with your aunties. Just a casual mention of Max made them latch on, and I could see the excitement lighting up their eyes, making them forget about the traffic and the heat. Now not even Regina could save me. I'd gone too far.

"Max?" Tita Fauna repeated. "As in a boy? Who is Max?"

Shit shit shit shit.

"*Hija*, I did not know you had a boyfriend!" Tita Merry exclaimed, turning around now to face us. The full force of their expectant looks was terrifying. "Was this the nice man you brought with you at the screening? I saw you two giggling in the back, I knew it!"

"Giggling in the back?" Regina asked with an amused quirk on her lip. She nudged me with her elbow. Oh god. "You go, Martita!"

Tita Fauna nodded solemnly from her place in the row in front of us. "That is very good to hear that you have a boyfriend, Martha. Honestly, I was getting very worried about you."

"Oh yes," Tita Flora agreed, whipping out a previously hidden fan from her purse to slap against the seat. "You know we were just about to offer you to stay with us in Pasadena, just so you can get your head together, make a plan. Maybe even lose weight..."

"We thought it would be a nice way to get you to finally find yourself a boyfriend. We have a few friends there with sons that are looking for a nice, fun girl to go out with," Tita Fauna pointed out. "Because we felt so bad that you haven't had one yet."

My back stiffened, and I noticed Regina making a face at the mention of the plan the titas had come up with. Sending me to California? Since when was that a plan? It was like I was being punished for enjoying my independence. I knew the aunts only meant well, but agreeing to that was acknowledging that I was unhappy with my life right now, and I wasn't!

"Well good thing I've already got Max! Ha-ha," I said awkwardly, feeling my stomach churn with acidity the moment the lie came out. I know it was a horrible thing to say, but it was only going to be a few events, and I could say we broke up when the wedding was over. We could totally pull this off, Max and I!

Did he even have to know? A little voice at the back of my head whispered. It wasn't like I was planning to bring him to any of the family events. I knew it would be weird. But the wedding, at least, I wanted to...

"Ma'am, are we stopping by McDonald's again?" Kuya Benj called from the front of the car, and I wanted to hit my forehead against the window and try to climb out. The aunts looked at me with a mixture of pride and pity.

"Oh she won't need fast food now that she's full with looooove," Regina sing-songed, and everyone started laughing all the way back to the house. I made a mental sign of the cross and apologized to God for my little white lie, but I was determined to keep this up. How hard could it be?

seven

The next Monday, I sat at my desk, tying up a status report for Max about his regular compliances, his permits, tax clearances and such while waiting for a few requirements we were looking for from Frank's company. They'd named themselves Very Efficient Developers, Inc., which was still not the weirdest name we've come across with.

I was also waiting for Regina to come to the office so we could go have lunch at a small place in Legaspi Village that did catering services. We needed to visit them since my usual caterer (I did this kind of thing a lot, if you couldn't tell) was already booked. This place was apparently one of the best kept secrets in the area, at least according to Mindy and Tita Flora, who recommended it.

I was listening to music in the background, absentmindedly humming along to the *Les Misérables* soundtrack while Mindy was working on her mails. She complained the entire morning how unfair it was that I had a legitimate excuse to go to the restaurant while she had to stay in the office and eat a salad 'like a Kardashian? Ew!'

I smiled and simply told her she was doing a great job. I liked watching her work. It was the first time I'd been assigned anyone, and to see her working hard and getting good results made me feel good.

Career-wise, I never thought I would do this for a living. A lot of people assumed that when I took a got my CPA license it was to put myself in the perfect position to inherit Dad and Tito Dennis' company. But I took up accounting because I actually liked it. People usually associate accounting with math, but to me, it was more like a language I had learned to become fluent in. The numbers told a story, and my job was to make sure people understood what the story was.

Dad and I have been talking about me finding out what I really wanted, and I didn't really have an answer. At least not right now. Although I did like my job, it wasn't something I was going to do for the rest of my life… was it?

My phone started to ring, and I picked up when I saw my Dad's extension number in the caller ID.

"Yes, boss?" I asked immediately.

"Can you come in please?" He asked. "Just for a minute."

"Sure," I said.

Philip Aguas, CPA, was a man who enjoyed efficiency. Dad lived by the rules of Six Sigma, an operations technique that contained guides and tools for general efficiency and improvement. He thrived on routine, and spent most of his time as managing partner finding problems in the office and trying to fix them, as Six Sigma dictated. He knew it was a thankless, endless job, but he loved it anyway.

"Hey Dad," I said, sitting across from him as he typed up an email. It took him a couple of minutes before he could refocus his attention on me.

"Hey sweetheart," he said. "I just got off the phone with Merry. Sounds like they're making this engagement party a pretty big deal, huh?"

I laughed. "That would be an understatement. They're talking about sending invitations to ambassador friends, and the who's who of Manila society! Who knew Tito Gerund's family was so up there?"

Well, we knew, because Tita Merry still lived in their house in fancy Forbes Park and only shopped within the vicinity of Makati. The fact that Regina lived in a large flat in central London alone was a pretty big deal. The Benitezes were one of the old rich families that only chose the cream of the crop to be a part of their family. I wouldn't be surprised if Regina's engagement appeared in the glossy pages of Town and Country or Metro Society.

Now do you see why being the one to plan this little engagement party was such a big deal for me? Regina even wanted us to have dresses made!

"Nah, it's your Tita," he said. "She's always liked the high society life. I think that's why she insists on you planning her events—she wants a protégé and an assistant. We were just talking about how good a job you were doing."

I frowned slightly, trying to guess where he wanted this conversation to go. He had that look on his face when he was trying to find problems. Oh my god, was he trying to Six Sigma me?

"Dad," I said testily. "What are you saying?"

"I just want you to be happy, that's all," he said. "I haven't really seen you smiling since you came off that stage in college, for the musical."

Trust my Dad to not remember the plot of Hairspray, but remember how happy I was about it. It was nice, but had I never really been that happy ever since? Was that why I was still holding on to Enzo in the most horribly inappropriate way?

"From the look on your face I can tell you didn't know until I pointed it out to you," he said, frowning. "Flora said you had a boyfriend? That can't be true, because you would submit the boy for your dear old Dad's approval, right?"

The question distracted me from thinking about my future, and for once, I was grateful. I smiled up at my father, neither confirming nor denying anything.

"Martha Ella Aguas, did you lie to your aunts?" He asked me, and I only gave him a more exaggerated smile in lieu of an answer. My father started to laugh, shaking his head.

"So you lied to save yourself," he said. "I have to admit I shouldn't be this proud. Does Max know that you're doing this?"

"Who said that I said Max?" I asked. My father gave me a look. Ack, he knew me too well. "I may never have to tell him."

"Sweetheart, knowing your titas, it's going to come up," he said, leaning back on his desk and chuckling. "Did Ate Flora say anything about her announcement? She's already been here for two days."

"No, she said she was going to do it when the whole family is together. Did Lydia know anything?"

"Nah. I'm sure it's no big deal. Now go to work. Think about what I said, okay?"

"Okay," I said, blowing my Dad a kiss, which he returned before I walked back to my desk to think about what I wanted.

* * *

What I Want

- EUROPE
- Milk Tea and fried tofu
- Korean food. Because bibimbap.
- Wagyu steak.
- Ugh where is Regina I am hungry.

"Martha," Jennie, the office receptionist, appeared by the door to pop her head into my office a couple of minutes later. I looked up from my pathetic list and blinked at her curiously. "I have a Mr. Lorenzo Miguel waiting for you at the conference room. He has those papers you were waiting for, and he says you have a lunch date."

"Wh—"

"What!" Mindy exclaimed before I could, bolting up from her seat. "You mean the Zac Efron lookalike from Very Efficient Developers? Oh my god! What is he doing here?!"

Jennie and I gave Mindy odd, confused looks. Apparently she was used to getting them because she still waited for her answers, waving her arms around and demanding explanations Jennie had already given.

"Er...he says he's here to take Miss Martha out for lunch," Jennie repeated. Mindy whirled at me, her eyes wide with shock. My eyes were pretty wide too, so we must have looked pretty hilarious.

"NO," she said like she couldn't believe it. "Really Martha? Two guys?!"

She smacked the table with her palm. "Damn, your pussy must be on fay-yah!"

I would have laughed if her face wasn't so serious, but I missed the reference and had no idea what that was supposed to mean. Mindy massaged the side of her temples. I knew this face she was making. This was her 'I literally can't deal right now' face. She paced in front of us and looked at me like I had three heads. She walked right up to me and placed both hands on the arms of my chair and leaned forward, angling her face way too close to mine.

"Okay girl, listen," she said to me. "I don't know how you do it, but by god, you have two crazy sexy men at your door. Plus, you've got boobs so big they could feed the universe. You are my goddess, Martha. You may not feel it in here," she said, waving a hand over my chest. "But you've got it in here," she continued, waving the same hand over as much of my body as she could wave her hand around. I wanted to laugh, but she looked so serious I didn't dare.

With a determined look on her face, she reached out and slightly loosened the French braid I'd meticulously done up that morning. She pinched my cheeks ('you need color!'), made me do a couple of mouth exercises to plump up my lips, and undid the top button of my shirt with a flick of the wrist.

"Mindy!" I exclaimed, as she pulled me up and ushered me to the door, saying how much of a relief it was that I liked wearing heels and tulip skirts to work. "He's my cousin's fiancée!"

"And when has that ever stopped anyone?" Mindy asked. "Now go out there and make me even more proud of you!"

Jennie sent me to the conference room where she made Enzo wait. He stood there, calm and cool like he couldn't hear my heart hammering in my chest or the loud clomps my fat feet made on the floor. He was looking out at the view, absentmindedly singing a song low in his throat. His voice rumbled, and I realized that I had missed hearing his singing voice. He was really good at it.

"...s'wonderful, s'marvellous..."

"That you should care for me," I sang, finishing the song and making him jump and turn to me. He smiled, and just like that I was in college again, looking into his eyes and telling him that he was the 'grooviest' guy in school for the musical.

"Hi," he said, and the dimple appeared on his cheek when he was being adorable and bashful. Wow, his hair looked fantastic in this light, extra floppy too. "Regina had to take Tita Merry to the dentist, so you have me instead. And I brought the files over."

I could feel my heart pounding in my chest. Why did he still have this weird power over me? I thought that after having sex with him, after leaving him the horrible way I did all those years ago it would go away, but it didn't. Not at all.

I smiled like it was no big deal.

"Awesomesauce," I said, and I wanted to bite my tongue immediately. "Nope, I did not just say that. Sorry. Shall we have lunch?"

"Lead the way, babydoll," he joked, coming up next to me. This wasn't healthy for me, I knew, since I just had a perfectly adequate sandwich and coffee with Mindy. But hey, this was all a part of the party planning experience. I might as well get a free meal out of it.

* * *

"Oh come on," Enzo said, poking his fork at the air in front of me. There were several plates of food in front of us, most of them empty. The restaurant was a hole-in-the-wall place in Makati's Legaspi Village, the kind you didn't know about until someone told you about it. Tita Merry apparently used to date the owner, and he owed her this one. Mindy was just very aware of secret places like this.

"I know you want the last of the Salmon Donburi," he said, pushing the plate towards me. "Come on Martha, we're friends. We can't leave a super-polite last piece of food."

Even though I was so full I couldn't eat another bite without popping another button on my blouse, I ate the last piece anyway. Like the rest of the food, it was delicious.

God, I was such a sucker for this. Enzo and I spent the entire lunch talking about the old days, the professors we had in common, the crazy things we did during rehearsals when we had shows and the weird rituals some of our orgmates used to have.

"...I swear I saw her sniffing his sweaty shirt," Enzo laughed, shaking his head as I grabbed my sides, more concerned over popping buttons than this hilarious story he was telling. "It was this smelly, threadbare thing, but she claimed it was a good luck ritual that he didn't know about."

"What! No way, that can't be right," I smiled, taking a sip of the water.

"It's true! Last I heard they got married and now she can sniff anything of his that she likes," Enzo joked, sipping his beer while I adjusted my skirt for what felt like the umpteenth time. Tulip skirts on my thick thighs were not made for eating long lunches.

When did sitting with a guy for a meal become so hard? It was never hard when I did it with Max (but that's Max, this is Enzo, my traitorous brain reminded me). But there was some weird tension in the air between us, an invisible rubber band threatening to snap at any second.

It was going to hurt like a bitch when it snapped.

"I do miss theatre though," Enzo sighed, taking another sip of his ice cold beer. It was his drink of choice in college, although this time it came with frozen froth that kept the drink cold. Like Enzo himself, he was still the same guy deep down, but with a sophisticated twist. "It's a different kind of rush, being on that stage, being someone else. Especially when you've been cast with someone awesome, say in a musical set in 1960s Baltimore."

I didn't miss the reference this time, and I wondered what the hell he was trying to say. I knew we needed to talk about what happened at some point. I knew I needed to ask if Regina knew about what happened between us, how he felt, what happened, what he was thinking now, why he was working for a building development company when he seemed so happy in theatre.

But I was a coward, and couldn't bring myself to burst the happy little bubble that formed around us, so fragile that anything could make it pop. What did Enzo want from me? What did I want from him?

"Hullo, darlings!" Regina exclaimed, and the bubble around us popped unceremoniously into tiny, useless soap suds on the floor. Her cheeks were slightly flushed from the heat, but she looked happy and totally excited to see us there.

Enzo, the perfect gentleman, immediately stood up and let Regina take his seat and sip his beer while he sat on my other side. "I wasn't feeling too well this morning, so I sent this guy," she said, squeezing his arm. "So you didn't feel abandoned, Martita."

I did mind, because Enzo said she was taking her mother to the dentist. But I said nothing, smiled and shook my head immediately.

"Nah, it's cool," I said. "We were just...catching up and stuff."

"Because you guys were into musical theatre, right!" She exclaimed, almost thrilled to recall that he and I had that connection. "I keep forgetting you did that whole Lea Salonga thing! I mean, Enzo sings his Broadway songs all the time, in the shower, in the car...but you've got a great singing voice too. I remember when we were kids you would sing 'Part of Your World' on cue because you thought you were Little Mermaid."

"Dude, I sang *Part of Your World* on cue because I *was* Little Mermaid," I joked, trying to find a way to diffuse the weird tension that was now trying to crawl its way up my throat. Or maybe I was just too full from lunch.

"Believe me, I was aware," Regina joked while Enzo laughed, raising a hand to ask the waitress for a cup of coffee.

"Really, Little Mermaid?" He teased, elbowing my very large arm. I watched my fat jiggle slightly before shrugging and owning up to my very weird childhood tendencies.

"Yes, throughout age five I would only answer to the name Princess Ariel."

"Oh! I almost forgot," Regina exclaimed out of nowhere, clapping her hands together as I hoped to god Enzo was not imagining me in a purple shell bra. "I just got off the phone with the florist. They said they won't be able to do the engagement party arrangements on such short notice."

"What?" I asked, whipping my head towards Regina.

"Apparently they already have a wedding to prep for that same week," she explained. That was a second supplier from my end that didn't deliver for the engagement party. I could almost interpret that as a sign from the universe, but I didn't believe in things like that, so I said nothing.

"What are we going to do? Everyone's going to expect a pretty centerpiece, and the caterer can't do that for us. And the photo booth! Remember, I wanted to do the wall of white roses, like Kim Kardashian? And what is a champagne and roses theme without actual florals?"

"Uhh...an engagement party?" Enzo dared to ask, and I immediately shook my head at him. I could see Regina was about to go into panic mode, so I said the first solution I could think of, even if it meant more things to do for me.

"Maybe we could ask someone to go to Dangwa, find the flowers we want there," I blurted out, already wishing I had bit my tongue. "I have a friend who's a freelance event stylist, maybe he can work something out."

"What's Dangwa?" Regina asked, blinking and pronouncing the place as 'deng-woh' with a slight British tilt to her tone. Even Enzo looked a little confused. I had to laugh. Then I said the five words I had promised myself I would never say for this engagement party.

"I'll take care of it," I promised Regina.

Upon hearing that I had come up with a magical solution to her problem, Regina clapped her hands and threw her arms around me in a hug, squeezing tightly. I saw Enzo look at me affectionately, and his warm smile nearly made me melt to the bottom of the table. The rubber band between us stretched again, raising the tension.

"Have you ever considered going into event planning, Martha?" Regina asked me once she'd released me from the hug. "I think you'd be amazing at it."

"Psh, it's just residual skills from being everyone's favorite front of house manager," I joked, and Enzo nodded solemnly. When I wasn't cast in plays as ensemble, I made sure I still joined in the background, just so I could get to watch the actors in their element, pick up things even if I wasn't part of the show.

Okay fine, Enzo being there was a factor, but only about half. Three-fourths, tops.

"I make a much better Little Mermaid than event planner."

"That's a pretty good Little Mermaid then, because that fundraiser event you arranged for the Metropolitan Museum was pretty amazing," Enzo pointed out. "The team told me you guys raised enough funds to arrange for some major repairs to the theatre."

"Wouldn't it be great if the theatre was fixed up in time for the wedding?" Regina gushed. "I've always wanted to see it. Mom and Dad used to go on dates there all the time, and it was so sweet. Oh, and speaking of dates," Regina said, smiling wryly at me and poking my arm as the dessert options arrived.

New York cheesecake, Devil's Food cake, Rose-infused buttercream, and candied violet cupcakes. Oh my god where has this place been all my life? I could eat here forever. Regina was only momentarily distracted, taking pictures of the sweets while I twirled my fork between my fingers, ready to attack. She put her phone down, and my fork was inches from the cake when she finally asked, "Are you bringing your boyfriend Max to the engagement party?"

Enzo started coughing as I put down my fork.

"Boyfriend?" he echoed, and Regina nodded enthusiastically.

"Yup! She confirmed it in the presence of the Aunties," Regina said. "And you can't lie in front of the Aunties. They can smell you lying and squeeze your nose until all the boogers come out."

"Oh ha-ha," I said to Regina. I had almost forgotten that I was supposed to be dating Max now. I hadn't even gotten around to telling him. I knew he would find this whole nefarious plan hilarious and play along, but I was hoping that because I'd already mentioned the existence of a boyfriend, they would leave me alone.

Apparently when you jump one hurdle in life, there were twelve others in front of you that you had to jump over too. I should have learned my lesson, really. "But I don't know..."

"No! Bring him, bring him!" Regina exclaimed, grabbing my wrist and shaking it, making my entire arm jiggle uncomfortably. "I want to meet this serial giggler. Ma's been trying to remember him, but there's only so much she could say beyond what she saw in a passing glance."

Enzo looked like he wasn't sure if he should be amused, surprised, or upset. I knew the feeling well.

"Come on now, don't let the family down, Marts," she said, picking up a fork and taking a huge bite off of the rose buttercream cake.

"Yeah, bring him," Enzo said gently. "It will be...fun."

Will it guys? Will it really? I scrunched my face up and stabbed my fork against the cake to stuff the dessert in my mouth to hide my frown. What the hell did I just get myself into again?

* * *

Later that evening, while I was catching up on work and finalizing the flower list that I'd coordinated with Tita Merry and the designer, I got a text from Enzo. Seeing as it was already one in the morning, the text surprised me. The only person who usually texted me this late was Mindy when she needed a car and Maggie when she needed Kuya Benjo to sneak out and pick her up without our parents knowing. The fact that I was listening to 'I Can Hear The Bells' from Hairspray was just a coincidence.

Enzo: So...boyfriend?? Must admit that was a surprise.

I bit my lip and looked down at Bibi sleeping in the small crevice my legs made when I sat Indian-style on the bed. I think he loved it because my thighs were always snug and warm while my feet were cold. He looked up at me curiously while I frowned at him.

"Should I reply?" I asked my dog, wise as he was old in dog years. Bibi was a master of nonverbal communication, and simply turned away from me to lay his head on my thigh.

"I'm taking that as a no," I said, rubbing the top of his head as I put aside my phone. I was not ready for any of this, so I just decided to go to sleep.

* * *

"Hey Max."

"Thank god you called, I really wanted to put that book down."

"You?" I asked in disbelief.

"Me. I've been in a bad book streak since…since the last time we talked."

I realized that it had been three weeks since that disastrous lunch at Tito Bob's Shawarma place, and three weeks since I talked to him.

Suddenly I missed him, which was weird, because I never used to miss him before. His Facebook was nearly silent (not that it was ever a reliable indicator of what was happening to him) except for George Torres' selfies with him (he rarely looked at the camera so she kept tagging #shybae on her posts), and her photos of him walking Wookie or carrying Tinkerbell the Bichon.

Not that I was keeping tabs on him, of course. Max was a grown man with his own life. I was busy with the engagement party, the wedding plans (the whole family was being roped in to that joyous occasion) and work to keep track of him.

So, anyway. I called him.

"Haven't heard from you in a while," he said casually, like it was no big deal to him. I swallowed a lump of hurt that had formed in my throat and tried to avoid letting it settle. It was early on a Saturday morning, and I woke up this morning with an urge to just pick up the phone and call him, like I usually did. Bibi's ears perked up and he wagged his little tail while sitting on my bed, like he knew Max was on the other end of the phone. I rubbed his ears.

"Yeah, well one of us is planning the social event of the year, with very little time for phone calls," I said jokingly, but the message hit home. I heard Max sigh. I could close my eyes and see him running his hand through his hair. Why was I trying to pick a fight with him? It wasn't his fault that I never called him.

"Martha," he sighed. "I don't want to fight. Now are you going to remind me to go to Mass tomorrow or am I going to pull my hair out trying to break my bad book streak?"

I swallowed my slight irritation and hurt and just asked him. Really, what did I have to lose?

"Do you want to drive me to Dangwa?"

There was a pause on his end of the line, and I wondered if he would say no. Did he even know where Dangwa was?

"Martha," he said, his voice low and serious. "I solemnly swear to go wherever you would like me to go on this fine Saturday morning. I'll pick you up in an hour."

"Wear closed shoes!"

* * *

That was how Max and I ended up starting off our Saturday in Dangwa. The drive was fun, we put on Aegis' greatest hits and sang all the way to the heart of Manila. Our concerto was only interrupted by the GPS on his phone, directing us to the right place.

"I haven't indulged in singing that loud since college," I laughed as we turned a street. It was a Saturday, which meant the traffic was instantly less horrific than it usually was. The roads of Manila were almost clear, save for a couple of crazy jaywalkers and street vendors. Max didn't seem to mind as much though, purchasing a couple of candies from a vendor on the street.

"You should do it more often," he said, keeping his eyes on the road as we turned into the right street corner.

I've known about Dangwa since high school. I studied in a Catholic, all-girls' school from first grade to high school, and in our senior year, we needed to buy flowers in bulk to learn the fine art of flower-arranging. I'm not kidding. My Home Economics teacher insisted we buy several stalks of azaleas and calla lilies and squares and squares of floral foam. I had green foam stuck under my fingernails for weeks.

Dangwa was a magical place, taking up the streets of Dimasalang, Laong-Laan, and Lacson Avenue in the middle of the city of Manila. Flowers were delivered throughout the day from the cooler parts of the country, and the bus stop was nearby, so the flower markets grew stall after stall of fresh flower vendors. Max looked a little surprised that the area even existed. Everything about it felt slightly makeshift, but the explosion of colors from all directions was a welcome sight amidst the layer of grime that settled over the city.

"Holy shit, where are we?" he asked, and I smiled at him knowingly as we headed in. The street we were walking on was slightly wet, since the vendors were throwing out old flower water on to the walking area. Thankfully Max was wearing closed shoes, as was I.

As with all Filipino markets, the assault on our eyes and the light tickle of the flowers was nothing compared to the shouts of the vendors who spotted a potential customer. I pulled Max gently by the elbow as left and right vendors started shouting at us. They promised imported Holland roses at fair prices, free flower girl bouquets if we ordered enough flowers, and azaleas sold by the kilo, which was a really tempting offer.

As we walked, men carrying buckets and bouquets of all shapes and sizes asked us to move aside to let them pass. Some of the walkways were taken over by large, muscled men in wife beaters artfully arranging flowers without batting an eyelash. Max and I walked past a man arranging a cascade of mums for a bridal bouquet when we found ourselves standing beside a bucket of bright sunflowers. I looked up at him.

"How do you know which stall to go in?" he asked.

"Oh, you've got a stray leaf there," I said, tiptoeing up to pull a bright green leaf from his hair. We'd passed by so many stalls now it was impossible not to get a little foliage on you.

"Thanks," he said, smiling down at me while I twirled the leaf in one hand. We'd been in such close proximity to each other, avoiding other people that seeing him right there in front of me was a bit...surprising. Possibly illuminating.

"Ay, look at that happy couple," the saleslady nearest to us said, pointing at me and Max from her seat underneath the awning over her stall. She had a portable electric fan over her sweaty face, and the radio behind her blasted the cheesiest of sixties tunes from the AM station. "So cute! They look like the perfect ten!" She howled with laughter, slapping the arm of the person next to her so see if they got the joke. "Get it? Coz' she's so fat?"

"I get it, they're like the numbers!" her companion said, and Max and I immediately turned to them with the most murderous of glares that we could muster. Did these women think we couldn't hear them?

"Hoy," Max spat out, and I realized I'd never heard him sound so annoyed. I'd never been openly teased like that in front of him, and he was taking it worse than I was. Was it because I was wearing a sleeveless top?

I backed down immediately. We were in their territory, and if Max decided to pick a fight, it wouldn't end well for either of us. Arguing with the florists was not going to help anyone.

"Who the fu—"

"You know, honey," I cut him off, placing my hands on his chest to cool his jets. The sudden intimacy of the touch made Max turn back to me in slight surprise. "We should probably move on. Five thousand stems of roses are not going to buy themselves."

Then I took his hand and pulled him away while the salesladies' jaws dropped at the business they had just lost. I didn't let go of Max's hand and looked up at him, once we were out of earshot, just to make sure he was okay.

"What happened back there, Rambo?" I asked. "Were you really ready to beat up a flower vendor?"

His frown deepened, and he shook his head. He looked down sadly at me, and I wondered if it upset him that he had to defend me because of my weight. "I just don't get why people have to make comments like that. It's so rude."

This new side of Max was utterly fascinating to me. Most of the time he acted like I was just a normal person, a bro he hung out with, or occasionally flirted with to make me squirm. Now he was being protective and concerned, it was...strange.

I knew I had to diffuse the tension somehow, so I shrugged.

"It's more fun in the Philippines."

"Really, Martha," he said with a sigh. "You don't have to act like it didn't hurt you, or that it didn't mean anything. You don't always have to smile and just let people walk all over you."

That hit a nerve, and he knew it. What was he trying to do?

"Well we can't all be sailing through life like you do," I said sharply, crossing my arms over my chest. His eyes widened, and I wondered how hard I hit on that particular nerve. I knew I was being neither logical nor fair. I wanted so bad to argue with him and yell, because to be completely honest, I was still a little angry about the way we both handled the George thing. We hadn't talked for three weeks, and I didn't like it at all. I ended up taking a deep breath, filling my lungs with the smell of warm, damp concrete and fresh flowers. I sighed.

"This is why we can't be together, Max," I joked, shaking my head. "You know me too well."

He smiled too, but I could tell he didn't find my joke amusing. We started walking together, now dodging passing vendors like experts. I peeked into the stalls, trying to find the kind of flowers we needed.

"I thought that would be my selling point," he said, following close behind me.

"Yeah, like that's the only thing I'm looking for in a relationship," I said sarcastically. "I just want someone who doesn't think I'm cute, you know? I'm too moody to be cute. Cute is what you call babies or chubby bunnies. Or an endearment you say when you want to tell someone they're ugly in a nice way."

"I don't think you're cute at all," he said immediately, and I squeezed his lower arm lightly. He faked getting hurt anyway, and it made me laugh. Max always made me laugh, and the little fog of anger above my head dissipated just as fast.

"So what's your number one requirement," I asked, as we continued our walk. "Maxwell Jeffrey Angeles's number one requirement for the woman of his dreams. Does she have to have read a thousand books? Be a dog lover? Listen to every band in the local gig scene?"

He paused, and I found myself holding my breath in anticipation.

"She has to be my best friend," he said simply, so sure of himself that I envied his confidence. "That's all you ever want in your person, right?"

I don't know why, but my heart fluttered and my cheeks burned. Who knew Max could be such a romantic? He's read so many books on love that he had to know. I smiled and looped my arms around his muscled arm so excitedly that my entire body bounced (boobs included) a little, making him sway slightly.

"You're exactly right," I agreed. "Now honey, are we going to buy flowers or what?"

At my use of the h-word, Max immediately lightened up. He curled his arm up (ooh, that bicep!) and clasped his hand against mine, kissing the back of my palm, before his lips quirked into a mischievous smile. There was the Max I knew.

"So we're really doing this?" He asked, raising our clasped hands with a quirked eyebrow. "Bring it on, boo-boo."

"Ew," I scrunched up my face at the sound of the name. "No, no. I don't like boo-boo."

"Honeybunch? Lovey-doves?"

"Max, those are horrible pet names," I laughed. I looped my arm around his, pushing him forward as he chuckled and tucked the same hand into his pocket. "What was the one that Elizabeth wants to be called in *Pride and Prejudice?* Goddess Divine?"

"If you're talking about that last scene from the movie version, I say it was totally unnecessary," he commented. "But I believe it was 'Lizzy' for every day, 'My Pearl' on Sundays, and 'Goddess Divine' on special occasions."

"And when she was truly, incandescently happy?" I smiled, looking up at him again. It was something I had done thousands of times before, but in this light, in this moment, in the rush of our laughter and the heady scent of the flowers surrounding us, it was dizzying and brilliant. Things had changed around us, and I didn't really understand it yet. But I knew it was nice, I knew it was easy. I knew I didn't want it to end yet.

Max, who knew the film version as well as he knew the novel itself, simply smiled and kissed my cheek with his lightly pursed lips.

"Mrs. Angeles," he said low into my ear, and I nearly dropped his hand in my shock. Instead I lost my footing, as I occasionally did and stumbled backwards into a bucket of carnations, nearly knocking it over. Max was quick though, reaching over my big and clumsy body to set the bucket upright before a single bloom fell out.

Behind us, the saleslady clapped his hands enthusiastically and started to laugh. A couple of the other stall owners looked on in amusement. I stood myself straight and smiled sheepishly. Oh my god if I wasn't blushing hard before, I was now!

"I am so sorry," I said to the owner. "I didn't mean to…"

"Oh relax dear, it was no harm, no foul," she said, smiling at us with her toothless mouth, waving her hand at me while she sat beside buckets and buckets of tall roses almost bursting from their stems. "Always nice to see a happy young couple in love. What are you looking for? All of these flowers are from Baguio, in my family's farm."

I'd consulted my list just before we left the car and I knew we were looking for as many roses as we could find, as well as white mophead hydrangeas, succulents, and the bright violet lily of the nile. I took a peek into the woman's store and saw she had most of the flowers we needed, some hanging upside down from the ceiling. Max had already wandered inside, looking at the flowers. His fingers reached out to lightly brush the pink sides of a stargazer. I would have thought he would be a little bored, but he seemed to be enjoying himself, touching everything like a kid in a toy store.

"Your family grows all of these?" Max asked, poking his fingers into a block of floral foam. "That's amazing. I didn't think you could grow these kinds of flowers here."

He indicated the hydrangeas, with their tiny white flowers clumped into balls that spread over big green leaves. The saleslady nodded.

"Hydrangeas are difficult to grow here, but they still do in our Baguio farm. They need patience and love, a lot of coaxing. But they always turn out beautiful, just as they are," she said, fondly smiling at the heads of hydrangeas in front of her. Max's face turned thoughtful as he studied the flowers, like he was trying to understand them himself.

"I need flowers for an engagement party," I said kindly, trying to be in charge. "Could you give me a quote for these?" I asked, showing her the list of flowers and the quantity we needed. I had an idea of the prices, and Tita Merry's approvals on how high I could go. They were planning on making a decadent wall of white roses for the photo booth, and that alone would cost tens of thousands of pesos. The aunts weren't kidding when they said they wanted this event to be big.

The saleslady's silver white eyebrows shot up when she saw the size of my order. I worried that she wouldn't be able to fulfill it, but she nodded and excused herself for a moment, walking over to the stall next door and showing her the piece of paper. They were talking to each other, pointing at flowers and nodding at each other. Max stood next to me with a bright, blue hydrangea bush in his hand. I had no idea when he picked that up.

"I have a question for you," he said, as we continued to watch them. "Pinky promise that you'll answer?"

"Okay," I said without thinking, twisting my pinky around his and wiggling it to make him laugh. He smiled, but it disappeared almost just as fast. Oh. He was serious.

"Why did you ask me to come with you today?" he asked, as the saleslady looked over at us and gave us a little wave to reassure us that she was coming back. We waved back, giving her the same smiles. I liked hers better because her toothlessness made her seem happier somehow.

As I dropped my hand I realized the answer didn't change. It didn't make my heart beat in my chest, or my hands turn clammy. The truth was never complicated or hard to say.

"Because I missed you," I said.

The saleslady returned with her quotation, offering to throw in a person to help with the floral arrangement, and delivery of the flowers. I threw myself into business mode and left Max to fend for himself, putting the hydrangeas back and plucking stems and leaves from random piles. Then he asked for some ribbon and plastic as Stella (the saleslady) and I finished the order and set the details. I promised her I would go to her for more events, and she seemed pleased.

"With this order alone, I can afford to spend a little more time at home," she told me, squeezing my hand. "That's all I really need."

When we emerged from the store, Max had a large array of flowers in his hands, and he was ecstatic to report that it cost half of what he would have had to pay if he bought it at the mall. I looked at the curious, mismatched collection of purples, yellows, pinks and oranges.

My Home Economics teacher would have disparaged his lack of leaves to support the flowers ("the flowers are jewels on a crown, ladies, not the gold that holds it together!") and the almost painful-to-the-eyes combination. The bouquet was bright, happy, spontaneous and a little silly, and it had Max all over it. I beamed with pride, but in the back of my mind I wondered if prim and properly put together George would like it.

"Here," he said, handing me the bouquet before I could think.

"Me?" I asked, my voice immediately rising. "This is for me?"

"Yeah," he chuckled as he started the car. "Because I missed you too."

I didn't want to tell him that this was the very first bouquet I'd ever received in my life, because I didn't want to freak him out. Why should it, though? He knows you better than most people do. I should feel sad that I got my first bouquet at 26, from my best friend no less, but I didn't. In fact, I wouldn't have had it any other way.

I buried my face in the flowers, inhaling their fresh scent. The petals touched my cheeks, and I smiled. I wanted this memory to be happy. I wanted to keep this particular memory close, because at the back of my mind, I knew that things between Max and I were changing, and I didn't know if that was a good thing or not.

eight

When Tita Flora decided to make her announcement, she grabbed the opportunity to turn it into somewhat a big to-do. She roped my mother into helping her arrange a "small soiree" with the family.

Anything she had to say, her daughter Lydia already knew, and there wasn't really anyone else to tell. My father had been right when he sensed it was going to be something big. Even Maggie was specifically asked to cut class to join us for the meal.

Dad always told me that he considered both Tita Flora and Fauna the heads of the family. Tita Flora was the sister who helped you get ready for prom, who taught you how to be cool and to sneak out of the house. Tita Fauna was the stern ate, the kind who asked if you did your homework or who gave you a hard time when you ask for allowance.

Because my grandfather used to work full time, Lola May took care of his needs while Tita Flora and Fauna watched over Dad and Tita Merry. I knew he was worried about whatever it was Tita Flora had to say, and I think this Tagaytay thing was just a way to ease whatever blow she was about to deal.

My aunt never did anything that wasn't big, loud, or floral. We shouldn't have been surprised, really. Mom rented a twenty-person event space for a crowd of about ten at Sonya's Garden in Tagaytay. It was Tita Flora's favorite place outside of Manila, because they served fresh salads and pastas with a slice of the most heavenly chocolate cake. Walking around the property was like walking through an English garden, or so Tita

Flora says.

I've always liked Sonya's, they had exotic flowers and bright, colorful blooms growing out of almost every possible crevice. The "greenhouses" that were converted into restaurants all had a rustic feel to them, with colored chandeliers and fresh greens every day. Mom and Dad used to drive here just to buy us bags of their specialty cheese hopia, crumbly and tart little rounds of pastry that flaked and filled your mouth. Ten bags with ten pieces each would probably last us a month. I was excited already.

This particular lunch was a joint thing between Mom, Tita Flora, and Regina. They coordinated with all the invitees and the garden, choosing a lunch and tea menu for the soirée. The only thing I had to do for this event was to show up, which was perfect because planning Regina's engagement party alone was already taking up too much of my time. I hadn't gotten a lot of sleep the night before after coordinating with the event stylist, so the only thing I was currently good for was ordering my family's ten packs of cheese hopia tarts from the bakery up front.

That was where Tita Fauna found me, talking to the cashier as I sipped on my iced Caramel Macchiato. The whole bakery smelled like fresh bread and butter, and I was already cradling a bag of cheese hopia in my arms.

"Martha," she sighed, tutting her head at my drink as she slid up beside me. "What do you have there?"

"Oh my god…Tita!" I jumped, and tried to keep my cool when I realized it was her. Tita Fauna was the stricter of the two aunts, her training as a teacher made her severe and seem a little controlling. But I knew she meant well, even if everything she said to me came with barbs. When I thought of evil stepmothers, Tita Fauna's face usually found its way into my imagination.

She pointed at my drink with her lips, hands on her hips. Oh boy. I'd done it now.

"It's iced coffee," I sad simply. "We passed by for some on our way here."

"Darling, that is a thousand calories that you're never going to lose," she said, shaking her head as she turned to the bakery offerings. I noticed her giving my ensemble a wary side-eyed look. What was wrong with wearing a fitted t-shirt and big floral midi skirt? I thought it was very girly and matched the venue. "You really should be more careful about what you eat. Really, you would look much more beautiful if you lost weight. Like Regina!"

She started laughing, and I bit my lip to hide my wince. Ugh. Tita Fauna really knew where to stab a bitch in the heart.

"Now tell me which of these menu items is that heavenly tart thing that your mother serves for merienda," she said, sidling up to me and acting like nothing had happened. I knew she thought she was being helpful, and I had to keep telling myself that repeatedly to believe it.

After helping her out and getting the cashier's reassurance that I could pick my orders up after the luncheon, I smiled weakly at her and told Tita Fauna that I would see her inside. That's when I saw Maggie sitting by a wooden bench in front of wild, showy dahlias, hunched over her phone, fingers flying fast.

"Help, I've been stabbed by Tita Fauna's words," I said, slowly collapsing next to her and spreading my body over her lap. I tossed my half-finished drink into the nearby trash can. Maggie rolled her eyes for my sake and put her phone aside.

"What was it this time? Your posture? Your breathing?"

"My caffeine addiction," I grumbled. "She said I would be prettier if I was thin."

Maggie put on a thoughtful look. "That doesn't mean she thinks you're not pretty now."

"Aw honey," I sighed, "You're sweet, but Aguas women are a little crazy and we know it."

We both shared a laugh. I sat up and she nudged my arm, brushing her skinnier elbow against mine.

"Ack, salvation!" Regina exclaimed, walking up to us from the entrance. She was wearing a very pretty romper, classy and playful at the same time. Her long, black hair was pulled back into a sleek ponytail, and anyone would have mistaken her for a model. Is that what I would look like if I were thin?

"Tita Flora just asked me if I was pregnant," she groaned, squeezing herself between me and Maggie on the bench. "Of all the nerve!"

Maggie, whose arm was placed over the back of the bench, suddenly reached out and tugged on a strand of my hair. I turned to her, and saw that she was giving me a look and pointing at Regina with her lips. I shook my head. Her brows furrowed. Her message rang loud and clear: if I wasn't going to tell Regina, Maggie would.

This is what I get for telling my sister everything. This was my opening. I took a small, calming breath as Regina continued her ranting.

"Is it because I'm getting fat?"

"Hey Reg," I said to her suddenly, trying to cross my legs. I couldn't, because of the size of my legs, and settled for crossing my ankles instead. "Why isn't Enzo doing theatre anymore? He was...he was so good at it."

Maggie suddenly bolted from the bench. Traitor!

Meanwhile, Regina frowned immediately at my question, playing with the hem of her romper shorts. Her ring sparkled in the afternoon light. I could tell she'd dodged this one before.

"His father died," she told me, "Just a year before he graduated from drama school. The theatre thing never sat well with Uncle Maynard, and Enzo felt he needed to respect his father's wishes so he came home and found a job with the developer. The owner is a friend of his father's, so he got the job quickly."

I never knew Enzo had that conflict with his father. I tried to recall him in college, trying to remember if his father had attended any of his shows. But everything was a bright, colorful blur of singing and stage lights and scenes, nothing stood out to me. He never told me anything about that, not in all that time we spent together.

"But is he happy?" I asked, looking at Regina. She bit her lip nervously, but it was a private expression, something I was probably not meant to see.

"I think he will be," she said, looking up at me.

Ask her. Ask her if she knows about you and Enzo. Ask her now.

"Actually," she said suddenly, squeezing my hand. "Enzo and I haven't exactly been getting along lately. We've been having...issues."

What?

"Regina?" Mom's voice rose from the inside the greenhouse we'd rented for the welcome home luncheon. "Can you come in and help me with the place settings? Your Mom said you would know who has to go where."

"Oh, yes," Regina said, immediately bolting up from her seat to follow the sound of Mom's voice. "I'll help you, Tita. Oh Martha!" she exclaimed, walking backwards as she faced me. "Have you gone for your fitting yet? Aling Rosing the dressmaker is buying the cloth next week, and she needs your measurements."

I groaned. "Reg, it's an engagement party! Why do I have to have a dress made?"

"Because I'm the bride, and I said so!" Regina exclaimed with a little wink. "Don't you want to be pretty for the society pages?" She asked before disappearing behind the door. I groaned again and pouted like a six-year old kid being made to stand in the corner.

I hated getting my measurements. There was always the seamstress' little tut of disapproval when she realized my stomach was nearly a whole measuring tape long. Having my body broken down into numbers just reminded me how far from the norm I was. I kicked at a rock on the ground, trying to think of a way to get out of it.

"What is the matter, Martha dear?" Tita Flora asked, appearing from the bathroom. She was wearing a flowy shirt with floral-print chiffon on top and lined with thick, blue fabric with her garish pink leggings. Trust Tita Flora to stand out in a garden full of bright and colorful flowers.

"Oh...nothing, Tita. I was just thinking," I said, giving her a smile as she sat next to me on the bench.

"Ooh! What about?" she asked, and started to fuss with my clothes, smoothing out my skirt and slightly lifting the collar of my shirt to hide my ample cleavage. I pulled at the front of my shirt a little, trying to get it to stretch out slightly. "Hmmm. Thank god we got you those new bras you ordered dear, that one is looking a little worse for wear," she tutted, shaking her head at my 42 DD cleavage. "You were thinking about your boyfriend?"

"Wha—No," I stammered. I nearly asked her what she was talking about, boyfriend, pish! I had once again forgotten that I was supposed to be dating Max. Tita Flora looked a little concerned and reached for my hand.

"Does he not want to marry you?" she asked me suddenly, taking my arm. "You tell me right now, because my announcement inside might change things for you. You're already 26 you know. I was 27 when I married my first husband."

ACK. I was just getting used to having a fake boyfriend, can we not bring in marriage yet? I shook my head at Tita Flora.

"No, it's not that, Tita," I promised her. "I wasn't..."

"Martha!" An all-too familiar voice exclaimed, and I swear my heart stopped for a moment when I saw him at the entrance. I had to be hallucinating, because this wasn't possible. But when he crossed the space between us and headed straight for a kiss on my cheek, I snapped out of it. "Surprise!"

He smiled at me, and suddenly time slowed and came to a halt around us. Everything was right in the world because my best friend was here! Weren't you supposed to be ecstatic when your best friend surprises you? I wanted to hug him. Him and the copy of Pride and Prejudice in his hands.

Questions raced through my mind, but none of them seemed important right then because Max was here! Right where I needed him to be, and I didn't even have to ask. Relief flooded me, and I smiled so much that my cheeks started to burn.

"Max," I said, and it came out so breathy that it surprised even me.

Then Tita Flora gasped, and I immediately realized my mistake. My little emotional high came crashing down as I remembered he was my faux beau.

CRAP. Why did I have to say his name? Now Tita Flora thought we were together! Be cool, be cool be cool. You can totally do this. Just. act. normal.

"You...you should really wear a jacket, it gets chilly at night up here," I said lamely instead. Max smiled, a tiny dimple appearing on his cheek as he assured me that he was fine. That he was actually wearing a light sports coat escaped my attention.

I was about to ask him what on Earth he was doing in Tagaytay (two hours away from Manila on a good day) of all places when Tita Flora gave the loudest, least subtle coughs known to mankind.

Uh-oh.

Her eyes were sparkling as Max and I turned to her expectantly. Her mouth opened, and I knew she was going to be asked to be introduced. I never realized what it was like to live in nightmares until that moment.

But before she could say anything, Max was already starting to speak.

"Hi, I'm Max Angeles," he said simply. "Martha told me she was going to be in Tagaytay all day with her aunts from the States. Tita Flora, I presume?"

"Yes," Tita Flora cooed, and I swear I saw her blush as she extended the back of her hand to Max for him to touch it lightly against his forehead in a respectful gesture. "Did Martha ask you to come today?"

"No Tita, I was on my way to visit a friend nearby, but it's a bit early, so I thought I would surprise her," he said, and they both gave my still slightly shocked face a cursory glance. "I think I managed to succeed."

"Oh you did, you did!" Tita Flora said excitedly, standing from the bench with the help of his gallantly outstretched hand. "Max, you must join us for lunch. I'm sure the rest of the family would love to meet the man who's swept our Martha off her feet! Have you met Regina yet? She's getting married soon to this wonderful man…"

The next thing I knew, Max was getting ushered into the restaurant as I watched helplessly from behind. From inside I could hear choruses of loud waves of laughs that rose and fell every few minutes. I slowly released a breath I realized I was holding on to. Max and Tita Flora were too busy charming the pants off of each other to notice my panic.

The room seemed to fall into total silence when they crossed the threshold. I could see Tita Merry's eyebrows furrow as she tried to remember why Max looked so familiar before she widened them in surprise.

Enzo dropped his phone. Regina looked at the pair curiously and gave me a look of confusion, no doubt to ask me who Tita Flora had brought in. Maggie's face crinkled with an evil little grin; we had a little bet about which of the aunts would become a cougar—I was betting on Tita Fauna showing off her wild side, and Maggie erred on the side of caution with Tita Flora. Even Lola May looked pleasantly surprised.

My mother, who already knew that I was faking all of this, smiled at me knowingly.

"Everyone!" Tita Flora announced like she hadn't already caught the attention of the entire room. "This is Max. He's Martha's....friend. Max, these are my sisters, my niece Regina, her fiancée Enzo, my mother and aunts, and I'm sure you know Martha's sister and parents."

"I had no idea this was a family affair," he said. "I wouldn't want to intrude."

"No, no stay!" Tita Flora exclaimed, squeezing his arm as she led him to a place they pulled up next to mine. We settled in our seats as Tita Flora walked to the right hand side of the head of the table--the place she always took at family gatherings. I saw Max frowning at someone from across the table and gave his legs a little kick when I realized who he was giving the evil eye to.

"What is your problem?" I whispered as Tita Flora clapped her hands to let the dinner service begin. Bowls full of salad seemed to materialize out of nowhere, with rose and marigold petals sprinkled on top. Butternut squash soup was ladled into our bowls. "Max, why are you so annoyed at Enzo?"

"He looks like the kind of jerk that would break your heart," Max whispered to me, nudging his head towards Enzo, who was sharing a joke with Tita Fauna about math, of all things. I felt the breath vanish from my lungs. His reaction was surprising and perplexing, to be honest.

"He already has," I said, reaching out to squeeze his arm. "Let's move on."

Conversation around the table was pleasant and easy, revolving around the three major topics that consumed the family. Regina's engagement party, the new Miss Philippines winner who turned out to be the niece of the daughter of the friend of someone Tita Merry knew in high school, and politics, when the conversation started going stale. This was all well and good for a normal Sunday brunch, but we all knew it wasn't.

From his place beside Maggie, I could tell Dad was getting antsy. Finally, at the end of the pasta course, my father turned his head toward his oldest sister.

"Ate Flora what is going on," he said, "Did we really come all of this way just to eat salad?"

Aunt Flora stood up and frowned at my father, a tiny bit of salad dressing left on her lip. Mom shook her head at my father, telling him to just calm down and eat.

"Since somebody here is so impatient," Tita Flora huffed, placing the tips of her hands on the table. "I am very glad you all took time to come here today. As you may have guessed, I gathered you all here for a reason. I would also like to welcome our guests, Lorenzo and Maximus…"

"Maxwell, his full name is Maxwell, Tita," I corrected her.

"Now Martha, it's rude to correct your aunt," he tutted at me, and I rolled my eyes.

"Nevertheless," Tita Flora continued, unperturbed. "I have an announcement to make."

"Just tell us, Ate!" Dad exclaimed. Clearly, the suspense was killing him.

"Philip," My grandmother said sharply.

"I have cancer, okay?" Tita Flora finally announced, so suddenly and so quickly that a sudden silence pierced the entire room. Lola June gasped. Max reached out and held my hand, and I squeezed it tightly.

From her place at the table, Tita Fauna grabbed her sister's hand much in the same way to support her.

"Fauna and I just found out. I have not been feeling well, and we had a doctor check a lump that formed. I'm at stage three, which is shocking, but I've already decided to just let it happen. However long it will take."

"But Flora…" Tita Merry began, already about to burst in to tears.

"*Hija*, certainly not," Lola April said vehemently.

But Tita Flora shook her head to stop anyone from interrupting.

"That being said," she continued, gesturing for everyone to lower their voices. "I've asked our attorney here to coordinate with mine in the US to prepare everything regarding my estate. Fauna and I live comfortably off the interest from an account in the US, and it now covers my doctor's fees."

"Once I pass away, that will go to her. There's always been money set aside for Lydia on her father's side. Everything else I made sure to divide up equally, and put into a trust fund for my three favorite kiddos, Regina Marie, Margaret, and Martha," she said, pointing her index fingers and wiggling it at myself, Regina, and Maggie.

Like the rest of the family, we could only stare at her, jaws on the floor.

"What does that mean, Aunt Flora?" Regina asked, lowering the hand she'd placed over her lips. She'd instinctively reached over towards Enzo.

"It means she's making you her inheritors," my father said, his brow furrowed. I could already see the wheels in his brain turning as he tried to think about what this meant for me and Marga—Maggie. "You placed it in a trust?"

"Yes, we've made sure it's set up in the US so it's tax free, like you recommended, Philip," she said. "And I've distributed it equally so that each of them will get…a hundred thousand dollars."

TITA FLORA SAY WHAT?!

Max actually did a spit-take of his soup, making Enzo cringe slightly. I thumped on his back while still starting at my aunt, who looked delighted at the prospect of shocking everyone this way.

"That's right, isn't it Fauna? Yes, yes, one hundred thousand dollars," she said, nodding when the more calm Tita Fauna confirmed the answer. She looked totally composed in these circumstances, which wasn't unusual for Tita Fauna. As the second daughter, she was always cool and level-headed, especially next to her dramatic ten-minute older twin. She must have had a lot of time to absorb it all.

"That's the prize money on *Drag Race!*" Maggie exclaimed, and I had to appreciate her ability to keep things in perspective. Next to me, Max chortled at the reference.

"Four million pesos," Dad said, as Mom gave a low whistle. "That's a lot of money, girls. What are the terms of the trust?"

Tita Flora had a large, cat-got-the-cream smile on her face, and I knew she wasn't going to make this easy for anyone. Her marriage to Uncle Helios, a Greek shipping magnate, had been rife with drama, and I think she found it fun to put us all through this. She wasn't just going to give the money, was she?

"Well, I imagine it will be very easy for the two of you," Tita Flora said, looking particularly at Regina and me, wiggling her eyebrows at the men. "And I made this stipulation because I want you girls to be happy and settled in life, so you don't have to think about money. You girls are smart and strong, and I have no doubt you will use this money wisely. I made this stipulation because I want to make sure you settle down and be as happy as possible. The trust stipulates that you must be engaged by midnight on your 27th birthday to receive the money."

I wanted to stand up and scream. Really. There was just…just too much going on. The only thing I knew about my life was that I wanted to see Europe. Tita Flora's will made sure that would happen, if I could do it. I was turning 27 in six months! If I was going to be engaged, it would be…

Max turned to me and caught my gaze with his eyes.

Oh my god.

I couldn't take the tension in the room, my knuckles turning white as I grabbed the arms of my seat. Suddenly there was a gap inside me, and I needed something to fill it.

You know what I needed just about then? I needed a cheese hopia.

"I'm going to the bathroom," I suddenly announced, pushing my chair back so quickly that it fell over backwards before I ran out of the greenhouse and headed straight to the bakery. One piece, I told myself, I needed at least one piece of cheese hopia.

"Martha!" I heard Max call after me, but I ignored him and continued to march right into the bake shop. "Martha Elaine Grimauldi Aguas!"

"None of those are my names, you dummy," I grumbled at him, handing my money over to the cashier in exchange for a bag of hopia. I tore the bag open and held it up to him for the sake of being polite. "Cheese hopia?"

"Let me take care of that," he said, grabbing the bag out of my hands and placing it high over his head, a space we both knew I would never be able to reach.

Then the idiot started running. Like we were kids in a schoolyard. I huffed slightly before I broke into a run after him, feeling every ounce of fat in my body jiggle as he stepped into a greenhouse marked 'Proposal Garden.'

The irony was just too much, but the space was undeniably beautiful. Deep magenta bougainvillea flowers cascaded from the ceilings like whimsical curtains. There was a full china set up in the middle, with rows and rows of deep red rose bushes leading to the table. Max was glaring at me as I struggled to catch my breath. He didn't look happy.

"What's gotten into you?" he asked. "Your Tita just announced that she's got cancer!"

"Yeah, but you heard the crazy rules about the trust, Max! I mean, everybody already thinks we're…" I said, biting my tongue immediately before I admitted that I had told everyone that we were dating.

Max's easy demeanor suddenly changed. He'd placed the cheese hopia on the table. Then his eyebrows furrowed before he crossed his arms over his chest.

Oh my god, he's giving me a stern look. The same kind of stern look I gave him all the time.

"Martha," he said, sighing deep and long before placing his hands on my shoulders, breathing deeply until I found myself naturally following the pattern of his breathing. The little ache in my stomach disappeared slowly. "You already work at a cool job, and you're almost halfway to your saving goal. Money is easy to come by. You've only got one Tita Flora."

I looked up at him again. When did Max become so wise?

"My friend was sick, some time ago," he shrugged in lieu of explanation. "It wasn't pretty, and I wished I could have done more for him. It's hard, Martha. A support system is the best thing your aunt has."

But he made a good point. Tita Flora was sick, and she probably came home to be with the family so we could help her through it. She probably thought she needed to create this crazy trust thing to "encourage" us to take care of her, which was why I couldn't focus on that. Max had already told me exactly what I needed to hear, I think. I would be an idiot to give up on the trust, but I would be a bigger idiot if I let it control my life.

"God, I'm horrible," I said.

"You're in shock," he corrected me. "Your aunt needs you, kiddo. This isn't about the money. And, just in case it doesn't work out, I solemnly swear that I will propose to you on your 27th birthday, and we'll blow it on a huge trip to Europe," Max promised. He raised his long, girly pinkie at me and started wiggling it, and I smiled and crossed it with my short, stubby one before he bumped the pad of his thumb against mine. "We'll stay at the Peninsula hotel in Paris, the prices are lower because it's legit haunted."

"So you'll only love me for my money," I pointed out to him.

"Yes, but I'll make a good husband, I promise," he said, giving me a little wink. "Now Martha Elaine," he said, picking up the cheese hopia from the table. "I'm confiscating these just so I can find out why you love them so much."

"Don't you dare," I said, reaching forward to grab it before he extended his arm backwards, the second place we both knew I could never manage to reach. "Argh! Worst husband ever!"

"Hey, you're still 26," he reminded me. "We're not getting engaged yet. And you could still meet someone, Martha. I know you will," he said, and for some reason, his smile turned a little wan, like it pained him to say all of this. "It's possible."

I managed to grab the hopia from him and took a bite. It was hard and bland, which never happened before. I frowned down at my food.

"Hey, which friend of yours is this?" I asked, following him back to the restaurant. "Have I met him before?"

"Oh don't worry, wifey, I'll introduce him to you soon enough," he said, taking another piece from the bag and taking a bite. "Damn, these are good."

The deal stood.

* * *

"There you are!" Tita Flora exclaimed, waving her raised fingers at us like we couldn't see her. Her bangles jangled loudly as we were led back to our seats. Regina gave me a concerned look, as did Enzo, but I shook my head at my cousin to reassure her that I was fine, and looked down at my plate of pasta. Max and I had eaten a couple of cheese hopias, and I wasn't hungry anymore.

"Now sit, sit!" Tita Merryweather exclaimed, asking the waiters to serve us our tarragon tea after their empty champagne flutes were cleared. "We've had some discussions about your Tita Flora's announcement. Obviously, we need a second opinion here. Luckily I have a co-member at the club whose husband has a cousin who is a very famous oncologist at St. Luke's. He should be able to tell us what's going on."

I turned to Tita Flora for confirmation, and she turned to Tita Fauna, who gave a small, almost imperceptible little nod. I could tell Tita Flora was scared without really letting it show, so I gave her a little reassuring smile.

"... and Enzo and Regina here have been talking nonstop. Now we want to know everything about you, Maxwell," Tita Merry finished, rapidly blinking at Max as a sign of her interest. He swallowed.

In my years as a member of the Aguas family, I have seen countless boyfriends and girlfriends cower and become terribly stiff and silent at a whole table of titas coaxing them to talk about themselves. Enzo, upon meeting my aunts for the first time, was all awkward, toothless smiles and polite nods. I should have known that Max would be different.

"Everything?" he asked. "I don't think I have enough champagne in me for that."

We all laughed, and his eyes met mine for a brief moment. I felt a small rush of love for him then, coming out of nowhere. It washed over me so pleasantly that I smiled at him.

"I am so sorry," I whispered low to him. He gave me a little wink.

"Just joking ladies, I'm sure a handsome Max has a couple of interesting stories up his sleeve," he said, rolling up the invisible sleeves on his arms and making everyone laugh. "Anyone here ever experienced birthing a giraffe?"

* * *

When the luncheon was over, the entire Aguas family started to walk back to the van while complaining about how much moist chocolate cake and tarragon tea we had. Meanwhile Max and Enzo were saddled with the giant paper bags of cheese hopia to bring to the car, much to Tita Flora's delight.

"Oooh I love it when pretty boys carry things for me," She cooed, and I saw Max's eyes widen suddenly after she passed him. I raised my eyebrow at him.

"She pinched me in the butt," he hissed at me, and I started laughing so hard I almost slipped on a rock, stumbling slightly.

"Kaaarma," He singsonged, and I tried to trip him with my toe, and he stuck his tongue out at him.

"Can you two stop being so dang cute?" Maggie asked, passing us and making a beeline for the car.

The family was already getting in, the engine was running, and Enzo was loading his two giant paper bags in the car. The amount of hopia we actually purchased was slightly comical, but my mom looked so happy with it. Lola May was already eating one.

Max adjusted the bags in his arms as we walked together.

"Did you really come here for me?" I asked him suddenly.

"I told you, I was meeting a friend," he said. "The same friend I promised to introduce to you. Scott just flew in from Hong Kong, and he wanted to introduce me to his girlfriend…"

"…Ava?" I finished for him, going on a hunch. His eyes sparkled at the coincidence, and I smiled.

"Yeah! How did you know?"

"Because I met Scott last night," I pointed out. "You should have come with us. He's cool. You met in Hong Kong?"

"Scotland," he corrected. "I'm meeting them at Bag of Beans tonight."

"Tonight?" I asked.

"Yeah, I drove up three hours early so I could come and see you."

The rush of happiness I felt for Max hit me so hard that I found myself tiptoeing up to him, careful not to let myself tip over as I smiled up at him and placed a light, gentle kiss on his lips with the entire family watching.

I swear I heard Regina squeal, and that was exactly what I was doing inside my head.

Oh god Martha, what have you done?

nine

"Just breathe, girl, you'll be fine," Regina reassured me a week later as we walked into the hair salon/design studio of Aling Rosing, the official seamstress of the Aguas family. There was a time when the Philippines wasn't RTW-ready, and older families still had their go-to seamstresses in hidden corners of Manila. Aling Rosing just happened to be Lola May's. She's been making ballgowns and everyday dresses for my aunts and grandparents since I was a kid. Lola May's wedding dress was still a thing of legend, framed and hanging in her bedroom.

One of the reasons why I didn't want to come over was because she knew I was having readymade dresses and clothes altered by a slightly less judgmental seamstresses in Kamuning. She commented once at the fit of my clothes when I last had something made, and I knew I'd aroused her suspicions.

But Regina was insistent, so insistent in fact that she came with me to the studio for the measurements session last week, and now was coming with me for the fitting.

Aling Rosing studied both of us, her eyes flying straight to Regina's waist. She tutted and shook her head as the measuring tape around her neck swished to the sides, but said nothing. Regina was having a Lhullier gown shipped from America, and Aling Rosing was in charge of making sure it looked custom made. I don't think she enjoyed that little delegation.

"I have your dress ready for you Martha," Aling Rosing said, squeezing my cheek before she led us into the back, with a pair of shearing scissors in her hand (oh my god she could stab me!). "I used the measurements from the last time you were here. Go to the back and try it out. Then I'll come for you."

"It sounds like she's going to murder me," I said, grabbing Regina's arm as she disappeared to the back. "Help me."

"You can do it," Regina said, pushing me forward.

Apparently Regina had this dress specially designed for me, to match the gowns they were having made for all the women of the Aguas family. Regina had chosen a happy, lemon yellow color for everyone, with the design being the variation.

The dress she designed for me had a fit bodice which fell straight down to the floor. The bodice clung to me in the wrong ways, hugging my stomach so it showed my underwear line and the canyon that housed my belly button, eurgh.

The dress was also too long, pooling on to the floor. On a regular person, a maxi dress would make them look long, slim and elegant. I just looked even shorter than I already was.

Then there was this cape thing. I'm sure Regina wanted to make me look avant-garde and cool, but I wasn't sure why she thought this would do it. It enveloped the top of my body like the cover of a birdcage, ending just above my elbows. I think it was a way to make my breasts look a bit smaller, but I felt it only made me seem frumpier. The absence of skin made me seem flatter somehow though.

But hey, the dress fit.

"Hey, can we talk?" Regina asked from the other side of the dressing room as I mentally disparaged over the dress.

"Yes, because this dress is—"

"Martha, do I really want to marry Enzo?" Regina asked, and that immediately sent me out of the dressing room, drape-y dress or no. I stared at my cousin in disbelief, and she just looked at me with sad and big brown eyes, her lower lip already jutting forward like she was trying her hardest not to cry.

"What are you talking about?" I asked her, lifting my voluminous skirt to walk toward her. Regina's arms were crossed over her chest.

"Hey," I said, rubbing her arm to comfort her. "Come on, Reg. Did something happen?"

She pulled away from my grasp, walking towards the window to glare at it a little. Now I was sure a flair for the dramatic was something we'd inherited from Tita Flora.

"Yeah, Tita Flora's inheritance happened," she said, shaking her head. "Money has always been an issue between us. He's got this idea that I don't work for what I have, that I'm used to everything being handed to me, while he's had to really bust his ass for it," she said, fingering the display of fabrics and haberdashery on Aling Rosing's work station.

"Then his father died. I told him he could stay in theatre if he wanted, I could support him, but that turned into a big fight that only made him push himself harder at that job with the construction company. Did you know they're having financial problems already? That last shipment nearly rendered them bankrupt."

This was news to me. Neither Frank, Enzo, nor any of his associates had breathed a word about it, and with the expanded witholding tax filing coming up, this wasn't something they should be hiding.

"Then Tita Flora made her announcement, and it was like we restarted the whole argument," Regina sighed. "We've been fighting about four million pesos, can you believe it? It's so stupid. I kept telling him it was a good thing that we will have a fund to start our lives with, and that Tita Flora could still live to ninety. But he doesn't want it, because we didn't work a day for it. What kind of a start is that?"

Tears fell freely from her face as we stood there in the room full of fabrics. I crossed the room slowly, coming to stand next to my cousin. I didn't know what to tell her.

To be honest, I understood what Enzo was trying to say. The wealth of the Benitez family wasn't something to take lightly, and it wouldn't be like him to just take Regina's charity and do what he loved. That wasn't in his nature. Why didn't Regina understand that? She'd insulted his ability to take care of her with that money.

But was that such a deal-breaker? I didn't think so.

So I did the only thing I could think to do, and hugged her. It seemed to do the trick, and Regina calmed down after a few soothing words. She'd been holding on to this for too long on her own, and I could tell that she just wanted someone, anyone, to know that this was happening.

I should tell her now. Now.

"You know, girl," Regina said as she rest her head on top of my chest. "Your breasts are amazing. They're big and soft and they can save the world. Seriously."

"Yeah, and everyone can call me SuperBoob," I said, making her chuckle and hug me tighter. It was hard for me to hug her back, what with my cape and all, but we made it work.

"By the way," I told her. "I hate this dress."

"It will look better after you wear the body shapers, promise," Regina said. "Love you, Martha."

"Yeah, yeah, love you too."

* * *

"Bathroom," I said to Max when I arrived at his condo a week later, pushing past him to make a beeline for his bathroom. I gave Wookie his customary head scratch in passing and let Bibi follow in behind me. I took the plastic carrying case with the dress with me into the bathroom. I heard Bibi bark and scratch at the now closed door for attention.

"Aww, Bibi," I heard Max coo on the other side of the door as I threw off my clothes, hung the carrying case on the hook by the door and brought out the dreaded underwear. I needed three layers of underwear before I could even consider putting on the dress. Tita Merry had been very strict about this. I hated to imagine what I would need to wear for the wedding. "Mommy is just taking a giant dump right now, okay? You can play with me and Wookie…"

"I am not pooping!" I explained from inside, shaking my head as I glared at myself in the mirror. "I have to try on this dress they had made for me, and your place is closer to the seamstress' than mine!"

Layer one was my standard underwear and panties. Check. Layer two was going to prove to be a little more difficult. I tossed the thing to the floor and placed my feet in the proper holes.

Now or never, I thought and pulled the thing up. I tried to pull it up in one smooth motion, but my own body kept getting in the way. Oh shit, it's tight. I huffed and pulled, twisting my body in the weirdest ways until I finally got them on with a sharp exhale of breath. I didn't even realize that was sucking in. I looked at my reflection in Max's mirror.

Is that what they were supposed to look like? Wearing the fresh-off-the-*balikbayan*-box Spanx was cutting off my breathing, even if it did pat down my stomach quite spectacularly. Who knew it was possible for me to have even a hint of an hourglass figure? I could see the slightest curve to my waist, and the bumpy points were kind of smoothed over to give the illusion that my body was quite shapely and slimmer.

Granted, it took a skintight pair of underwear to achieve, but I had to admit, the overall effect was nice. I exhaled deeply. I had to wear a minimizer over my bra, and that wasn't pleasant either. I moved quickly and in short gasps of breath, threw the lemon yellow horror of a dress over my head and opened the door.

"Why does it sound like you're about to—"

"Ha-ha, funny guy," I interrupted, walking out the door with one hand over my presumably smaller breasts to keep the dress from falling. I exhaled a low breath, and I could hear Max's breath hitch. "Zip me up?"

I heard him swallow thickly as I offered my back to him. I was already anticipating the number of ways this dress was unflattering for me, just based on the way it looked on me and covered me up entirely when I tried it on at the fitting. Where was the cape thing?

I looked down and realized I was wearing a completely different dress now. It dropped so low in front that I was sure my grandmother wasn't going to approve, and rose up to the nape of my neck in the back. The sleeves were now made of the same lightweight chiffon that formed the bottom of the dress, showing off skin without displaying my large arms.

Now I could see why I had to wear so many body shapers. When had Regina done this?

Max released a low, even breath but did nothing. Why did he seem uncomfortable? I looked over my shoulder and up at him, furrowing my brows in confusion. Why did he look so...surprised?

"Darling, I know I've got back rolls, now please zip me up," I sighed, pulling my hair back and holding it up with my hand so it didn't get caught in the zip.

I felt his hands on the small of my back, one sliding over to my waist while the other slipped slightly to my back where the Spanx ended. The touch was warm and light, and the fact that I could still feel it under three layers of underwear was surprising.

Max pulled up the zip slowly, using the hand on my waist to keep me steady. For the first time in my life, the zipper ran smoothly up my back. I guess the underwear did help. His fingers hesitated just at the top of the zip, like he didn't want it to end.

"Martha," he said with a low voice. "Why did you kiss me that day in Tagaytay?"

I inhaled a sharp breath. I hadn't forgotten what I'd done that day, but Max had been so caught with entertaining everyone that we never had the chance to talk about it.

"I was happy to see you," I said lamely, lowering my hands as Max finished the zip and rest his other hand on my waist. "I'm always happy to see you."

It was the truth, and the truth, when matched with his hands on my waist and his breath tickling my neck made everything warm and electric. Max seemed to hesitate before he came closer, heat prickling at the points where our skin met until I felt his lips place a light kiss on the side of my neck. I should have jumped, I should have pushed him away and said that this was weird.

But I didn't want to.

This, out of all the things I've felt in the last month, actually felt right.

"Max," I said in a whisper, as his hands snaked up the side of my dress before pulling me close to him. "Are you sure you want to do this?"

He laughed and buried his face against the crook of my neck and shoulder (how he managed to find that, I don't know). The laugh rumbled against my skin and made me feel all warm and tingly. His arms wrapped tightly around my waist, his fingers just managing to meet in front of my stomach and I took a step backwards, squeezing my hands over his arms to keep them there.

"Martha," he said, kissing the point on my neck where he'd left his laugh. "I've wanted this for so long. I don't... I tried to find someone else..."

"George," I said, the reminder of her settling in my stomach like a rock.

"I really tried, Martha. But she wasn't you," he said, and the words settled on my skin, making me shiver. "She didn't make me happy the way you do. I ended things with her the day before you called to take me to Dangwa. For once in my life, the timing was right, and you were there. I was ready to keep this, just for me, to let you go because I didn't know if you would," he said.

I turned around, making his fingers separate from their precarious hold on me.

"But now you're here Martha and I'm...I'm over the moon."

He chuckled as I smiled, and he placed a quick kiss over my lips. His eyes were hazy and dreamy, as if he still couldn't believe it. Neither could I, really.

"I cannot fix the hour, or the spot, or the look. It was too long ago and I was in the middle before I knew it had begun," he said, brushing a hand over my cheek. I knew the quote by heart, and it was like he had opened my eyes to what I'd been unable to see for the last few days. I kept asking myself what had changed between us.

And then I knew. It was me, because I finally looked and saw Max.

I rested my hands on his chest, feeling his heartbeat drumming from within. Both our eyes were wide and hesitant, but the excitement hummed between us.

"But..." I said, not really sure why I wanted to ask him this. "...why? Look at me Max, I'm not...I mean, I know I'm okay, but I'm not exactly the girl of your dreams."

When I said that, Max simply smiled.

"I told you Martha," he said. "The only thing she has to be is my best friend. That's you, and nobody else, gorgeous."

I don't know why him calling me that made my knees buckle.

"Plus I heard you were coming into quite a lot of money," he joked, and where I usually would have told him to piss off, I lowered my head to hide my laugh. I don't know why I did that either. But I did know why I tiptoed up slightly to kiss him. In the back of my mind, I was sure I was going to lose my balance, but his hands gripped my waist to steady me. It felt so wonderful to know he would be able to steady me, to anchor me as we kissed. He tasted like mint and toothpaste and possibilities, and the closer he came the warmer my body felt.

The world, in that moment, was a perfect place. I couldn't have enough of him. His hand rose up my back to the point where the dress was zipped up around me, and I was hit by a quick bolt of panic. The room was too bright, and if Max took off my dress now, he would see everything. Every bit of cellulite, every stretch mark and varicose vein, every jiggle would be exposed, and it terrified me that my own body had the potential to chase him away. Suddenly nothing else mattered than keeping all of that hidden away. I pulled away from him, and his eyebrow quirked at me curiously.

"Uhm..." I said, knowing how ridiculous I would sound. "If we're going to do this...maybe we should turn off the lights. Draw the drapes. Everything. And we should be maybe lying down. Can I take off your shirt? I feel very naked right now," I stammered suddenly, pulling back.

To his credit, Max didn't look at me like I was crazy at all. He simply took my hand and led me to the bedroom, where all the blinds were still closed, books scattered in every corner imaginable. It was so dark that I knocked into a couple of piles as we made our way to the bed. He stood over me and bent to kiss me again, and I pulled his arm down. I was so ready to pull his shirt over his head.

"No, no, wait," he said, and now it was his turn to pull away, walking to the ensuite bathroom to turn the light on and leave the door ajar, creating soft mood lighting. He smiled at me again, and I could feel my insides melting. "I need to see you."

He bent down so our lips could meet. His hand traced the nape of my neck to my spine, clutching the zipper where it kept the dress up. Then he pulled it down, chasing the exposed skin with his other hand as he unzipped the dress. With a small tug at the hem, we let The Dress (as I would forever call it) drift to the floor.

"How much underwear are you wearing right now?" he laughed.

"Well, something has to hold all of this in," I said, indicating my body. "Hey, don't laugh, you know it took me forever to get this on!"

"And now you're going to see how fast I can get it off," he said to me, flashing a mischievous little grin. In the dim bathroom light, he almost looked like a sly fox, so close to what he wanted that he couldn't help but rub his hands together. I wasn't about to take that away from him.

We kissed again, and any vestige of worry and insecurity I had evaporated quickly. In Max's arms, I was sexy and gorgeous, and the kisses he placed on my neck seemed to sing my body praises. Then his hands started to wander, and my entire body stiffened. This was it. Once I was naked in front of him, there was no turning back, was there?

The minimizer flew off before I knew, revealing the full size of my breasts squeezed into to a lacy pink bra. Even Max seemed surprised at the size of them, especially when he cupped one in each hand. I stifled a little groan, and pulled his face up to give him a kiss.

"You're moving quite slow, Max," I teased, pulling his shirt up and off his body in a quick, deft movement.

* * *

The last time I had sex was the first time. Back then, it was all about just getting it over with, because I honestly thought the secrets of the universe would open up to me when I did. Everything was hurried and we were both slightly drunk, and I just wanted to get it done.

Of course the universe remained as mysterious as it always was and the floodgates that held its secrets stayed stubbornly shut. Adults should really tell you that they know just as little about the universe as you did.

Max and I were both sober, and it felt like we had all the time in the world. We giggled when our teeth smashed together, or when I pulled his hair too hard. When I lay down on the bed, I'd propped up a pillow low on my back so my boobs didn't split off in different directions or fall into my neck. Max smiled, and in an impressive display of strength, grabbed my arms and flipped us over, and I was above him, looking into his dark eyes.

"I've Googled this," he said proudly, rising slightly to kiss a spot on my throat. "I want you to love this, Martha. I mean really, really enjoy this, so we can do it again…and again…"

"You perv," I laughed, steadying myself with a hand near his head and shivering as each word he repeated was punctuated by a kiss on my breasts. Laughing, he reached for a condom from his bedside table.

My breath caught in my throat, but it was more from anticipation than worry. I should be panicking. I should be closing my eyes or running away, because of the "no mating policy". But it was the last thing he and I wanted right now. Desire hit me so hard and quick that I didn't want to process or think about what was happening. I just wanted Max. I desired him, and god, if he wasn't going to move faster…

Our hands touched when I reached down to help him along. The tips of his fingers were cold, and his dark eyes burned into mine as his lips curled into a mischievous grin. I never noticed that his teeth were crooked before. A flush of bright pink lit up his cheeks and his neck, and my heart melted.

I raised myself slightly over him, already feeling the muscles in my arms shake.

"Wait!" He exclaimed, tightening his grip on my arms. "Count to three?"

"What?!" I exclaimed. "Max, I can't hold myself up for too long…"

"I've got you," he said simply, raising his hips. I squirmed when I felt him against me, and my entire body tingled. "One…"

"Twothree," I said quickly, and oh my god we were having sex. My insides immediately tensed up, and god, I hated to sound like a cliché, but he filled me up so well. I could feel my pulse beating against my temples as Max moved underneath me. Every muscle in my body was burning, but I didn't want it to stop. I raised my hips experimentally to meet his and Max actually threw his head back, exposing the long line of his neck. I bent down to kiss his throat, and he gave out a strangled cry. Holy shit we were actually making sex noises!

Then his hand clasped firmly behind me and pulled me down. I had no idea feeling this good was actually possible. The universe was opening up all of its secrets to me, but I was having so much fun with Max that I didn't want to listen. All I wanted was to be here with him, and keep letting him do that thing he's doing with his hips.

"You have no idea," he said, his hands pulling me down on him as my arms grew tired. My elbows were on the bed, holding me up because I didn't want to crush him. The muscles in my core clenched and my entire body shuddered. The next time Max bragged about his abilities in the bedroom, I was never going to doubt him. "How long I've wanted you like this, gorgeous."

He kissed me, hot and fierce, and I squeezed my thighs in response. But my body was starting to feel too heavy, muscles I've never used protesting. I balled my hands into fists, pulling myself away from a kiss to steady my breath.

Max sensed my discomfort right away and pulled me close, letting himself sink deeper into me before he rolled us over, gravity on my breasts be damned. He started fondling them, licking one of them at some point, but I barely noticed. My knees rose naturally and my toes curled as he pushed in deeper, my head pushing backward into the pillow. The more we moved the more my body tensed, and the more it did, the happier I felt. This was exhilarating!

I tried to move in counterpoint against him, but I couldn't move fast enough to match him. Lowering a leg gave me room to grab his moving hips, to slow him down so I could keep up. I wanted Max to enjoy this too.

"Oh Martha, you are amazing," he purred, and he beamed down at me before a little twist of my hip made him groan so loudly that I couldn't believe it was coming out of his mouth. "Fuck, that's good."

"How can you look at me like that?" I asked, screwing my eyes shut and stretching my neck back. "How can you look at me and not see my body?"

Max kissed the hollow of my throat. He grasped my cheek, making me open my eyes. From where were were lying, I had the perfect view of his incredible body. I could see the sweat that glistened off his brow. I could reach out and feel the tension in his neck, dipping down to his collarbones, and trace a perfect line to the flexed abs on his long torso. His arms were thick and tense but strong, supporting us both as we moved together, like a wave slamming against a concrete wall. Guess which one I was.

He kissed me insistently. Passionately, like he was trying to wash away my little joke. He gave me a stern look and pulled back. I felt him slipping out, opening my mouth to complain when he thrust forward, kissing my neck.

How could I be with someone like him? How could I possibly hope to make him happy? I bit my lip and arched my back. Max pulled me back, resting his forehead against mine. He closed his eyes, and his lips were inches from mine. They were slightly swollen. I realized, with a thrill running up my spine, that I did that. that I could make him feel like that.

He was gasping for breath, slightly sweaty and smiling as we slowed the pace, like he wasn't the one that couldn't keep up. I made him feel like that.

"I can see your body. Every line, every curve, every mark," he said, lifting his head. He ran his hand down my neck, my cheek, my breasts, my stretch marks, tracing the same path I had imagined on his body. "And it's perfect."

I really couldn't blame myself for kissing him so suddenly that my head nearly smashed into his.

Things built to a crazy pressure in my head fast, and I was moving muscles that had never been touched before. I did my best to move against him, because it just made things so much more delicious. It felt like we were running, racing towards the edge of a cliff with our hands clasped together and my heart pounding in my ears. My eyes were squeezing shut no matter how badly I wanted to look, to see, and the tension coiled deliciously between my legs. Was this what it was supposed to feel like? A rush, things pounding, muscles burning and heat building? It certainly didn't feel like this the last time.

I didn't want to think about what this meant for us on the other side, how our friendship would change. All that I knew was how this felt, how sensual and sexy he made me feel. After all, it felt so.very.good.

"How am I...still...breathing," I said, in between gasps, and Max lost his rhythm for a moment, shifting positions again. The little ache building in my muscles eased up, and I managed to raise my legs and squeeze my massive thighs against his sides, encouraging him to drive deeper. My eyes were wide open now, and I forgot to be insecure about my body.

"How...are...you...still...talking?" he asked, and it was my turn to go off balance, kissing the nearest bit of him I could grasp, with a smile on my lips as he lowered his head against my neck and...

"I love you, Martha," Max whispered.

Everything exploded and I released the tightness that had coiled inside me. Nothing else was left, just his body against mine, and this fantastic feeling that just felt...mind-bogglingly, earth-shattering, happily-ever-after fantastic and sexy and gorgeous. My entire universe was this white hot light that had burst from inside, and I weighed absolutely nothing.

The next thing I knew, I was scrabbling for something to hold on to, gasping, finding him and pulling him closer as my entire body shuddered uncontrollably. I could hear Bibi and Wookie barking from the other side of the bedroom door, and Max...Max's dark eyes watched me as I fell, chasing the feeling with feather light kisses to my jaw. Did he finish? Did I just...

"Oh my god," I said, laughing as he gently fell on top of me, his hand taking care to support his weight as we both gasped and wheezed and laughed. The world was bright, shiny, and happy. There I was, lying in bed naked with my best friend. "I didn't know it would be...I mean..."

Max immediately pushed himself up to get off the bed, and walked to the wastebasket where he discarded the condom, his bare back to me. My eyes traveled low on his ass and I wanted to laugh. I'd squeezed that. And when he turned around, I closed my eyes while he laughed at my attempt to preserve his modesty.

I swallowed thickly. I had no idea how toned his body was underneath those shirts, how much power he could have over an immovable force like me. It was surprising and wonderful.

He slid into bed next to me, and I instinctively cradled his head on my arm, his head resting lightly on the spot between my shoulder and breasts. I remembered thinking that lying in bed in the morning was the sexiest I would ever feel. I was wrong.

This, lying in bed with Max quietly as I caught my breath? This was the sexiest I've ever felt.

ten

I listened to our breathing for a while.

It took me longer to catch my breath than it did him, which sucked because when I tried to listen to us breathing all I could hear was my own wheezing. Neither of us wanted to speak, to break the spell we were under.

Wookie realized that the door was actually ajar the entire time Max and I were inside, and now he and Bibi were curled up at our feet on the bed. I buried my face in his chest, smiling. I couldn't help it. This was better than any coffee commercial fantasy that I could come up with.

"Are you okay? Anything hurt?" he asked, scanning my face and body like he was expecting something to be bleeding or falling off. I shook my head.

"I'll probably be sore in the morning," I said, already feeling it in my arms, my thighs. Even my back was a little achy. But right now I could be bleeding somewhere and not have it ruin my high.

Oh my god, I get the appeal of sex now.

"I guess you weren't kidding when you said you were good at this, then?"

"Would I lie to you, gorgeous?" he joked.

"You would," I laughed, poking his bare chest. His dexterity and strength had surprised me. Who knew he had abs under those t-shirts?

Max feigned getting hurt before he kissed my forehead. I raised my eyes to his, looking deeply into my sleepy, languid gaze.

"Hey Max, did you...er..."

"Does it matter?" he asked nonchalantly, like this sort of thing happened to him all the time. "It wasn't about me."

"Oh," I said, and let the silence stretch on. I hummed a song from Cats as I played with his hair, my mind still half in shock and my eyes fluttering. Max was still looking at me.

"Martha," he said seriously, his fingers brushing up and down against my thigh as I curled it over his. His massive hand still wasn't enough to envelop it. "I meant what I said. I do love you."

I opened my mouth to speak, but he beat me to it.

"And if you don't feel the same, or if you want to keep this between us… nothing has to change. I swear I can be cool about this."

I quickly sat up and clapped my hand over his mouth to shut him up. His hand was halfway up my thigh.

"Max, it's a little late for that," I said, smiling before I smacked my lips over my own hand. "I'm not too sure about how I feel yet, but I know that I enjoyed this."

He mumbled something from underneath my hand and I dropped it to let him speak, pulling his bed sheet up to cover my breasts. If he noticed my sudden modesty, he didn't let on.

"So much that you'd like a repeat performance?" he asked, wiggling his eyebrows at me.

The suggestive gesture made me roll my eyes, which naturally wandered down to the apex of his thighs. Oh my god, how had I not noticed that before?

"If we're going to do this again," I said, pulling the sheet with me as I walked up from the bed, stumbling slightly. Yep, I was going to feel this in the morning. "I'm going to need water."

I let Max's laughter follow me all the way out the bedroom, where Wookie and Bibi followed me curiously, their heads tilted to the side as they played with their toys. My bag was still in his living room couch, so I pulled out a pen and a notebook from it, tearing off a sheet and scribbling something on the torn page.

Then, with the dogs still watching, I picked up one of Max's books

(Stardust by Neil Gaiman) and slipped the note inside before I returned the book to the shelf.

"Don't tell Max," I whispered to them before I walked to the kitchen, with Bibi trying to hop on to the hem of the blanket.

Max would tell me much later that he could hear me laughing all the way from the bedroom.

* * *

I came in to the office the next day in a chipper mood. I smiled at everyone who greeted me, and I found myself humming my favorite showtunes as I walked into the office. As soon as I walked in with a cup of energizing morning fruit shake, I saw Mindy's head snap up and study me from tip to toe like she was scanning me for weapons.

"Oh my god, you've had sex," she said point blank, immediately dropping everything to wheel herself right in front of me in her office chair.

"Good morning to you too," I chirped, skipping past her to walk to my desk while singing under my breath.

"Martha!" Mindy squealed, rolling next to me again, this time slamming her hand on my desk like it could keep me there. "Tell me everything!"

"We've got a lot of work to do, Minds, the senior accountants will want support for the tax filings," I said with a tiny smile. "Plus I have to leave early because of this yoga thing Tita Merry signed us up for. Although I will confess that I had a pretty great weekend."

She squealed, reaching a decibel I knew only my dog could hear.

"Oh my god! You are such a fertile goddess!" she exclaimed, so excited she was bouncing in her office chair. "I knew your boobs were big for a reason!"

I accepted the compliment for the first time. Then, for some odd reason, Mindy, my co-worker and assistant, started rubbing my arms and fondling with the fat on my detached earlobes. It tickled, so I laughed and pulled away from her.

"What are you doing?"

"What does it look like? I'm rubbing you for good luck!" She exclaimed, and I laughed and convinced her to go back to work, checking my phone when I saw a series of text messages from Max. I snorted.

Max: Miss me? Come over tonight. I'll let you feel my bicep. Or maybe more ;)

Max: Okay I stole that from *Friends*, but appropriate.

Max: Your Tita Flora said you used to refer to yourself as the Little Mermaid. I will need instant confirmation, possibly a photo if this is true.

Martha: I am neither confirming nor denying and wth are you doing talking to Tita Flora??

Max: HA. So it is true.

Getting into work mode was always easy for me, although it did feel like a chore more than anything else. I was responding to client emails, helping Mindy work out the math to figure out the proper authorized capital a ten-million peso startup needed before I got another text. This time, it wasn't from Max.

Enzo: Want to show you something amazing. Meet me? Tell everyone it was urgent.

Wondering what this was about, I told Mindy I would be out to lunch to meet with a client (not exactly a lie), and took my car to the address he sent me. I found myself in front of a large warehouse, just at the edge of the business district right next to Pasig River. I wrinkled my nose slightly from the smell of the dead river and found Enzo waiting for me by the door.

"This doesn't feel very amazing so far," I told him, and he laughed and pulled my hand to the door like a kid in a toy store. I'd never seen him so excited.

"Trust me, you'll like it," he promised, as we entered the warehouse itself. The place was teeming with life--workers yelling at each other as large structures were moved from one area of the room to the other. Things were being unloaded from a container van, and I remembered why Enzo was so excited. We'd processed the shipment of Very Efficient Developments goods, and the container had just come into the warehouse.

"I wanted to show you what we were planning to do with all the things you helped us set up," he said, practically sprinting to the middle of the warehouse. "The fruits of our labors, so to speak."

We stopped at a clearing, and I furrowed my brows, confused at what I was looking at. It was a house. Nicely made, and quite spacious, it stood proudly in the middle of the building. Enzo's grin was wide as he looked at it, his pride overflowing.

"It's a house," I said, looking at it.

"Yeah, it's a house that took us only twenty days to build," he said to me with that little grin he had that always made the girls go crazy. "That's what I do here for Frank. He developed these 'House in a Box' projects, and I find a market for each of them. This model is the one we're looking to offer for victims of calamities at low rates. Earthquake-proof up to intensity 8, and flood-proof too."

He walked towards the house, and I could see pride in every step he took. His shoulders were raised and he wore his chin high because he knew he'd done good work. I approached the house with him, and had to admit, it was impressive. They were going to use this as the model house, he explained to me, and they'd added all the furnishings and fixtures inside.

I stood inside the house, looking around. Was I surprised that Enzo managed to pull this off? Maybe. But that smile on his face was hard to place. Had observed him so closely that I knew when he was acting and when he wasn't. He was acting right now, for some reason. It's not that he wasn't sincere. He just didn't seem all too convinced about what he was doing. I folded my arms over my chest and studied him carefully. He smiled at me.

"What do you think?" he asked, crossing one foot over the other to make a small spin around the house. "They're also developing these sorts of pre-made things for classrooms. The high end models will help pay for these ones, and we'll be set."

"I think you're going to make a lot of families in Tacloban very happy," I said. "But why are you showing me all of this? All I did was set it up, you made all of this happen."

"You helped me work on this," he said. "I couldn't have done it without you."

I remembered Regina talking to me about her fights with Enzo over money. Was that why he was trying to show me this? Because he knew that I would appreciate it?

"I was just doing my job," I pointed out to him. "You don't need to make this about anything else."

Then came the first real look on Enzo's face. He frowned and looked pensive, looking down at his leather shoes as he scuffed the floor with them, his hands in the pockets of his trousers. He looked like a poster from a movie, in this lighting.

"Why are we acting like nothing happened?" I pressed, leaning against the kitchen sink. I knew I was being cruel. Something had been unleashed in me, and finally, finally I was talking to him. I wasn't afraid of consequence, or of upsetting him. I needed to say this, before it got way too complicated.

"Enzo, we haven't talked to each other since college. Now you're acting like I matter to you. All we had between us was that one play decades ago, and one night. I was gone the morning after."

"Believe me, I remember," he said, looking at me like I was the one who had hurt him. "Why didn't you stay?"

"And then what?" I asked, pushing myself off of the kitchen sink. "The play was over, you were heading off to London, what would have been the point? I left because I knew it didn't mean anything to you. It was just sex."

This time, he looked up. He was hurt. Like I had been the one who gutted his heart out and left it on display for everyone to see. Like he was the one who had been in love.

"How could you possibly know that, Martha?" he asked, shaking his head in disbelief. "I really thought we had something back then."

"That's crap," I said to him before I walked off to the bedroom like a coward. I sat on the bed, trying to regain my breath. I knew we needed to have this conversation, but it was difficult. It had already been way too long, and my feelings had flip-flopped all over the place since he came back. Where was he four years ago?

"Not crap, it was the truth!" Enzo said from behind the door. It didn't lock, so he could have come inside, but I think he needed the space and the distance too. "I told you I remember everything about that night. I saw you leaving, and a part of me wanted to get up and fight for you to stay. Sometimes I wish I did, because I was in love with you, Martha. I was so in love with you. I can't believe I let you go like that."

I leapt up from the bed. Suddenly the entire room was suffocating, and my heart was hammering in my chest. I needed to breathe, but I seemed to have forgotten how. Everything had fallen away, the world was right side up, and I was left standing there with nothing but a pre-fab door separating me from him.

The door swung open, and I actually took a step back. He was giving me the look I wished had given me all those years ago. He wasn't acting, and if I had been the Martha from a month ago, I would have been the first one in line to grab his face and kiss him like there was no tomorrow.

"Enzo," I said to him in warning. "You can't say things like that."

"Why not?"

"Because I loved you," I said to him. The words spilled out of my mouth before I could stop them, like the beads on a necklace that had snapped. They scattered everywhere, and it was impossible to catch them all now. I'd been holding it together for too long. "I have, long before that night ever happened. I was just so scared you would reject me, and I didn't think…"

His eyes widened, and the shock of those words seemed to shake him as badly as it had shaken me. He was so close that the heat from his body radiated off of mine, warming my toes and burning my cheeks. The fire around us started burning so hotly that I needed space to breathe. Was this what being in love supposed to feel like?

"What about…what about Max?" he asked me.

I had this image in my head how this was supposed to go. I would tell him the truth and he would smile and cradle me in his arms. Then he would kiss me, and I would feel so light and happy that we would actually start floating while 'As Long As You're Mine' from *Wicked* would play in the background.

But this was nothing like that at all. Instead of feeling freed of the feelings I've been harboring for so long, it was like someone had piled on more weight to them, and I was dragging it all over the ground. I felt horrible and guilty, and I wanted it to go away. All the heat and the warmth vanished immediately, washed out suddenly by a bucket of ice cold water.

My feelings for Enzo were gone, just like that. What happened? I'd been holding on to it for so long that I didn't notice when it left. We didn't bother to fight for how we felt, so anything we could have had, the possibility of him and I, vanished in wisps of smoke.

"Martha," he said gently. "What about Max?"

"Max isn't my—I mean, we…" I stammered. "We're just…"

Hunger rose from inside me in the worst way possible. My mouth craved for something sweet to fight the bitterness hanging above us. I knew it was wrong. This moment was going to leave a permanent, gaping hole inside me if I didn't stop it now.

"Enzo," I said, placing my hands over his chest to push him away. "We can't do this."

His face changed, like he was trying to hold in a laugh. Of course he knew that we couldn't do anything. It was way too late for both of us. We were done.

"Of course," he said. "I'm marrying Regina."

"Yeah," I said, sighing deeply. "And I'm….not."

He smiled. "Are you okay?"

"I don't know," I shrugged, putting distance between us. "Does Regina know what happened at the cast party?" I asked him, and he shook his head.

An alarm rang from my phone, telling me I had to go if I wanted to get to Tita Merry's on time. I pushed past Enzo and he followed me out of the house, out to the factory. I heard him calling my name, but I ignored it. I walked so briskly that my thighs began to burn, and I was panting by the time I reached the car.

He reached me easily, placing his hand over the door before I could reach it.

"What are you going to do?" he asked me. I frowned at him and used all of my weight to push him aside and get in and lock the door. I lowered the window just enough so he could hear me.

"I have to go," I said, and started the car. "We have this yoga thing…"

"We should have said something," Enzo said.

"I don't owe her anything," I told him. "But I should have told her the day she came home."

The last thing I saw on my rear view mirror was Enzo's face pale and I drove away from him, and away from the feelings that I had known for so long.

* * *

When I arrived at the Benitez house, everyone was already in position for the yoga class. Apparently Tita Flora found a guy who offered to teach them yoga at home. Maggie was the most enthusiastic of us to do it, standing in front in her fresh from America Lulu Lemon yoga leggings and skintight tank top. Regina was wearing something similar (although she opted to wear a sports bra instead of a shirt), and they were taking a selfie. Tita Merry was sitting on the mat, chatting with her sisters, who were chittering about how nervous they were to have things stretched. The teacher hadn't shown up yet.

"Oh Martha, you're here!" Regina exclaimed with glee, bouncing over to me with her ponytail. "Isn't this cool? I had no idea you could do home service yoga."

"Yeah," I said, feeling slightly jumpy. "I'll just change in the bathroom."

"Okay, hurry back, we're starting soon!" Regina exclaimed.

I nodded wordlessly and headed straight for the bathroom, taking a second to catch my breath. The knowledge of what I'd done was pressing down on me. I couldn't help but feel that Enzo was just going to burst into the room and tell everybody that I'd declared my love for him and that my relationship with Max was a sham.

I was guilty, and I hated the feeling. I knew I was going to say something, and soon.

I changed quickly and emerged back into the living room. Maggie and Regina were waiting for me by the door, both of them giggling like mad.

"Holy quivering bodice, Martha! You might want to leave something to the imagination boob-wise," Regina said, raising her hand to the sports bra I was wearing, deliberately placing her hand over my chest.

"Oh, stop that, she looks great!" Maggie shushed her, pushing me back towards the living room. "Your mom is wearing sweatbands and a headband. I don't think my sister's fantastic boobs are going to be bad for anyone."

"Regina, I slept with Enzo," I suddenly said, clapping a hand over my mouth. Oh my god, since when was I a word-vomiter? I was fat! I should know a thing or two about keeping things inside, goddammit!

Her hands immediately dropped from mine, and she stepped back like I was contagious. Maggie's eyes were bugged out in surprise. I've seen Regina seethe, but I've never seen her do it like this. Her back was ramrod straight, and her eyes shrunk into tiny slits.

"What?" she asked me.

"It was a long time ago," I prefaced. God, I should have started with that. "Back in college. I told him that I was in love with him, and—"

"You're in love with him?" Regina exclaimed, like that was the worst part of what I had to say. Maggie, who knew nothing about all of this, could only look between us in shock.

"I told him this afternoon," I said in a small voice. I was going to run out of words soon. "I was in love with him for so long, Regina. I couldn't keep it inside anymore."

"That's bullshit," she yelled, the curse word making the whole house vibrate like it disapproved. "If you were so in love with him, why didn't you say anything? I've been here for more than a month now, Martha! There were literally dozens of times you could have said something. Even then you should have told me the moment you saw him get down on one knee for me!"

This was a fight I was never going to win, I knew. It didn't stop me trying, though.

"It wasn't easy, okay?" I said. "He brought up a lot of unresolved feelings when he came back, and I wanted to work them out for myself before I told you!"

"That's a lie, and you know it!" Regina yelled back. The accusation cut through me, especially because I knew she was right. I wanted to keep my feelings to myself. I wanted Enzo's attention, I wanted our friendship to become this thorn on the side of her relationship, because I thought I wanted Enzo for myself.

I have never been so wrong in my entire life.

"Ladies, what's going on here?" Tita Fauna asked, emerging from the other room. She was still in her house dress and slippers, and I knew she had heard every word we'd said.

"For once in your life, stay out of this, Tita." Regina snapped. She'd always had this mean streak to her when she was a kid. She used to be an expert at making me cry, scratching me, calling me names when I had done nothing to deserve it.

But now for the first time, I knew she had every right to say horrible things to me.

"So if you were so in love with Enzo, what was Max, then?" she asked, hitting me right where she knew I would be vulnerable. Her words pierced me like knives, leaving me bleeding.

"What?"

"Oh come on! It's too late to be the innocent, insecure one here!" Regina continued. "What was Max? Did you use him to get the money, because God knows you're going to need it when Tito Philip retires next year!"

What? When had Dad's retirement ever been on the table?

"Max had nothing to do with this—"

"Just answer the question, Martha!" she said, picking up a small figurine from the nearby console and throwing it at my feet where it shattered into a thousand tiny pieces.

Tita Fauna shrieked, and sent the rest of the house running, including Tita Merry, Tita Flora, and most inexplicably, Max himself.

What the hell was he doing here?

He was wearing a pair of shorts and a sleeveless shirt that said 'Yoga Manila'. Oh my god. He was the yoga teacher. No wonder Regina was so concerned about my boob exposure.

My heart stopped and started to wrench until there was nothing of it left. I felt so exhausted suddenly, and I just wanted this horrible thing to be over. I was crushed into a corner between Regina's angry face and Max's confusion. Tears streamed down my face, and I knew that I deserved this. But he didn't. Max had done nothing, and now I had to…

"We're just friends," I said, dropping my face into my hands. "Max and I aren't together."

I couldn't bear to see that look on his face, and I was too much of a coward to look.

"Coming back here was a mistake," Regina said, and I heard her scoff. "Just get out of here, Martha. I don't want you here."

That was it. It was one thing for her to fight me when I was coming to her, but it was another to kick me while I was down. I raised my head defiantly at Regina and pulled my hands away from hers, rising to my full height when I faced her.

Regina look gutted, her face slightly pale as she looked at me. I made sure to look like I wasn't breaking inside too. Then I said the one thing that would officially turn this fight into the shit storm of the year.

"Just…count me out of your engagement party. I don't want any part of it. I quit."

"Because you're in love with the groom?"

"No," I said, glaring at Regina. "Because I can't stand one more minute of you."

Then I walked out of the house with my hands shaking and my stomach cramping. I needed to get away from here. I managed to make it to the car when I heard footsteps running towards me. I knew who it was before I heard him call my name. My fingers gripped the car door handle, and I took a deep breath, willing myself to keep upright.

I was out of tears, out of words and I wanted to collapse to the ground. I barely had anything left in me to fight, I couldn't handle this right now. I covered my mouth with my free hand, willing myself to turn around, breathe and face him. Could I do that?

I stood still when his footsteps stopped. I was tempted to laugh and tease him about being a yoga teacher, but we were so far past that.

"Max, please," I whispered. Maybe I was praying. "Don't...I can't—"

"You can and you will," he said sharply, forcing me to turn and face him when he grabbed my shoulders. I wanted to leave, but he kept his hands squeezed on my arms until I looked him right in the eye. I couldn't breathe as the guilt and pain weighed down on me. I was gasping for breath in between my tears.

"You lied to me."

"No! I didn't!" I cried out, immediately wanting to crumble and fall, but Max wasn't letting me. He wanted me to face this now, in my cousins' garage after I barely got out of there alive. Couldn't he see I how hurt I was? Did he have to gut out my heart too?

"Max, I never meant to hurt you—"

"What the hell was that, then!" he exclaimed, and I had never, ever heard him so angry. "We could hear you from the living room! You know how I felt about you, and you said, you said..."

His voice trailed off as his face grew pale. For a chilling minute, Max stood still, and my heart stopped. When did he ever stand still? Even when we watched movies his leg keeps shaking when he crossed it. To see him absolutely still was terrifying.

"Oh my god," he finally said. "You didn't say anything, did you?"

The realization seemed to hit Max like a slap in the face. I said nothing, but I could see his mind racing a mile a minute, recounting everything I said to him, every moment we had together. He'd laid his heart out to me, and I…I said nothing.

"Shit. Shit. I am such a fucking idiot. You didn't say anything! Oh my god," he said, shaking his head. Max started pacing wildly in front of me, running his hands through his hair, rubbing over the beginnings of stubble on his chin. "For fuck's sake. You must think I'm the biggest idiot."

My lips remained closed. I was out of words and declarations. I just wanted this to be over.

"You should have just told me, Martha," he said, and I realized he wasn't doing this because he wanted me to face it. He was doing it because he wanted that pain he was feeling to stop. He was trying to 'deal with' me, and he was trying to get this over and done with. I couldn't handle that. I tried to reach for him, but he pulled away. I knew I'd already hurt him too badly. "That you didn't want…you can't lead me on like that, that's not like you at all."

Fresh tears sprung to my eyes at that, and I really, really just needed to hold him. I could bring him back if I could just tell him the right thing. What was I going to do if Max was gone? Who was going to make sure he went to church? Who was going to make sure he ate right, and bought groceries?

Who was going to help me?

"Please let me go," I said. I needed time to regroup, I needed time to sort everything out, and for me to do that, he had to let me get into my car and drive away.

But apparently that was the worst thing I could have possibly said. Even Max looked shocked. His hands dropped from my sides and he took a step back from me.

Without looking at him, I turned to my car and went back in. I managed to drive as far as the village gates before I pulled over and laid my head on my hands that still gripped the steering wheel to cry my eyes out.

My mouth was dry and my stomach was empty, but all I wanted was to go home.

eleven

My father and I were silent as we cut into our slabs of Wagyu beef a week later. The fats of the meat sizzled against the hot marble plate, sending oil splattering over our hands, our clothes. Light jazz music played over the speaker as we occasionally sprinkled salt over our food. Waiters came by our table to refill our glasses with the Cabernet Sauvignon Dad chose from their cellar.

Above our heads, an exhaust fan whirred discreetly to remove the meaty smell from the restaurant. We even had fancy bibs to keep our clothes clean.

It had been a week since the incident at the Benitez' home. News of my fallout with Regina reached my family before I walked through the door, with Mom and Dad trying to find out more details about what happened.

I'd managed to keep mum about the whole thing, throwing myself to my work. I had no idea of how my little blowup had changed anything for the happy couple—I was being conveniently kept in a news blackout. Mindy even offered to take me out to drink my problems away.

I didn't need a drink, I needed a good, rare Grade 9 steak. I needed something moist and juicy to chew on, because it may just help ward off this horrible guilt I felt. There wasn't anything I could do to get out of this, because it was my own fault.

The reminder of my own helplessness made me stab my mashed potatoes.

"Your meat is going to get well done," Dad pointed out, reaching over to move my steak around the stone to stop it from cooking too quickly. "And we both know that you might as well eat rocks if you're eating steak well done."

I frowned at my food, slicing off another piece of steak. Sawing into the meat would have helped my aggression, but the steak just split apart like butter.

God, this steak was good. I could eat this steak forever. I would enjoy that more than having to endure another day feeling like crap.

"Martha," my father said, squeezing my hand. "Are you okay?"

"Me? " I asked, my voice rising to a weird pitch like it did when I tried to lie. "Of course, I'm totally....not."

I finally sighed, resting my elbow on the table to give my double chin a spot to lean on. "I'm sad. The steak isn't working."

"A good steak can't fix anything but a craving," Dad pointed out, as he took a sip of his wine. "And a craving is only a symptom for something else. You're not happy, Martha."

I put down my fork and fixed my father with a glare. He's been thinking this for some time, I know. If he's bringing it up again, it means he doesn't think it's been fixed.

"Dad," I sighed. "I don't want to talk about —"

"I'm not talking about Regina or Enzo, sweetheart," he said. "You haven't been happy for some time now. Is it...a weight thing? I know your mom and I tease you quite a bit about it..."

I made a dismissive noise.

"No, it's not that," I said, picking up my fork again to cut up some more steak before I put it in my mouth. I could see Dad giving me an incredulous look as I chewed, and it took all of the soft juiciness of the steak away.

"It's not a weight thing!" I exclaimed in exasperation after I swallowed. "I'm actually happy with my weight, even though it's hard to believe. I like that I can work it, because it's mine. Everyone makes me feel so guilty for it, like there's something wrong with me. But come on. I look amazing. And honestly? I don't say it enough. I LOOK AMAZING."

There was a quick moment of silence as the restaurant heard my little declaration, but it was the truth. For all my whining and complaining about my body, it was mine. I owned it, and I owned it proudly. Dad nodded solemnly at me, and I knew he believed me.

So why was he still trying to Six Sigma me?

"It's not a weight thing," My father conceded. "But it's something. The last time I saw you smiling was—"

"I know, I know, my college musical," I sighed, taking my knife and fork to cut into my food. I looked over the table to find my father chuckling at his steak. "Believe me Dad, if I knew I could be the next Idina Menzel, we wouldn't be having this conversation."

"Nope," he said like he was the smartest guy in the world. "I was going to say the last time I saw you this happy was that day in Tagaytay."

"Well, I learned I could potentially inherit four million pesos, so…"

"No, before that," he sighed. "When Max and Ate Flora walked into the room. You looked so happy to have him there."

I knew I must have looked ridiculous, staring at my Dad with wide eyes, not even realizing that I'd dropped my fork on the marble slab.

It's weird, the moment you realize you're in love. You see it when you've lost it, and at the most random, inappropriate of times. Because the moment I cut into that steak that afternoon, I realized that I was in love with Max. I didn't recognize it at first, because I'd known love to be this slow, agonizing thing that was never returned.

But this? This kind of love filled my heart with so much happiness that I wanted to laugh.

I was in love with Max.

I loved him like I loved waking up on Sunday mornings. I loved that I could collapse on his furniture without worrying that it would break, that I could smile and just be myself with him. I love that he never asked me why I was so dependent on food, but instead forced me to look at what was really wrong.

I loved that he was there whenever I asked him to be, that he let me take care of him even if he felt smothered sometimes. I loved the way he smiled when he kissed me, the way he made me feel when we were together.

And I let all of that go for what? An illusion of a guy who clearly loved someone else?

I wanted to curl into a ball and sob out all the pain. The big girl never gets the guy in romantic comedies anyway. It would be much easier for me to give up and let him fall in love with girls like Georgina Torres, who could actually run with him and keep up with his constant motion and not have her boobs pop out of her sports bra.

It was easier, but it wasn't what I wanted.

I looked over at my father, who had already finished his food. He was studying me again. I hated it when he tried to fix me, but I knew he did it because he only wanted me to be happy. He wanted me to find what I wanted.

"Are you really retiring, Dad?" I finally asked him.

"Yes," he said. "Before I retire, I want to try and find a place where you belong. Although I think we both know where to find that."

I put down my knife and fork and smiled at my Dad before I kissed his cheek. My heart may be breaking, but I knew it would work out in the end. He squeezed my shoulder. Somehow I'd lost my appetite for steak, even the Wagyu beef kind.

Who was I kidding, that steak was too good not to finish.

* * *

It was strange. I thought that when I told Enzo how I felt I would want to see him fight for me. I thought I would look for him or cry his name into my pillow every night or think of him whenever I heard a corny hugot line. I don't know why I thought love would be so painful. It only hurt because it was wrong. Enzo might have been mine for some time, but that was over now.

Truth was, I didn't even think about him until I walked into the conference room for a meeting and saw him there. It was a regular Tuesday, and on a regular Tuesday, I was late to work and too worried about my lipstick to notice it was him until I closed the door behind me.

"Hi Frank, I—" I said, blinking as my brain processed his presence.

"I know you'd usually bolt from this kind of thing," he said. "But please don't."

I said nothing, but stayed. His face was dark and serious, and I had never seen him like this before. One of his old critiques in college was that he lacked range—you could tell when he was mechanically putting on his 'mad' face, his 'sad' face or his 'glad' face. I had no idea what this was. "What are you doing here?"

"I came to see you," he said without a hint of kindness or warmth in his voice. "We need to talk."

"I think we've talked enough," I snorted, crossing my arms over my chest.

"I meant talk about what happened between you and Regina," he said, still and unmoving in front of me. I shot him a look of annoyance, stopping just short of rolling my eyes. "I know you told her," he continued. "And she was angry at me for some time because I didn't say anything. But she needs you, Martha. She can't handle this event on her own, it's too much for her."

"Oh but it wasn't too much to ask me despite the fact that I work full time here?" I asked, waving my arms around. "I find it hard to believe that poor little Regina could possibly need me to handle her own damn event."

Enzo's face was inscrutable. God, his range had really improved in drama school. Then when I still said nothing, it slowly gave way to confusion, then realization.

"She didn't tell you," he said bluntly. "Oh."

I blinked back at him. I couldn't help the rush of concern I felt for Regina, no matter how hurt I was or how angry I was at her.

"She needs you because she's dealing with something too," he said. "Tita Flora."

I blinked at Enzo, like the words just flew right past me. He had a little smile on his face, the kind of genuine smile that used to make my heart twist inside my chest. Now I was just confused.

"Tita Flora? She said she was doing well so far, considering," I pointed out to him.

"Regina spent some time taking care of cancer patients," Enzo said, tucking his hands into his pockets. "That was how we met. We were performing for them, she was volunteering. She isn't dealing with your Aunt's illness very well. She knows what will happen, and she's not sure she can stand seeing it happen to Tita Flora."

I bit my bottom lip but let Enzo continue.

"I know this sounds like crap, but that's why I've picked a fight with her over this money thing," he said. "It hasn't been the easiest for us, me struggling to do well while she needed me less and less," he shook his head.

"But anyway. You're going to have to support each other more and more, and better now than never."

I lowered my arms.

"So this is me, begging you to patch things up with her. You calm her down, and she needs calm right now."

I blinked up at him. Enzo gave me a tiny smile, like he understood my little non-gesture completely. I had to admit, I was impressed by him. He came here despite knowing what happened, just to beg me to help Regina. He knew that we were going to have to see each other eventually, and just sloughed on. It helped a lot, because my plan had been to avoid family events totally. With this, I knew where we both stood on the matter.

"I know you'll think about it," he said earnestly. "Now I'm going to leave," he said. "You can act like we never talked."

He saw me nod. Then he crossed the room and left. This is what we were going to be from now on. It wasn't the happy ending I wanted, but it was one we could accept.

Twelve

AGUAS FAMILY SECRET GROUP

Maggie Aguas created the group.

Flora Aguas has joined the group.

Fauna Aguas has joined the group.

Merryweather Aguas has joined the group.

Philip Aguas has joined the group.

Chari Aguas has joined the group.

Fauna: Hello family. Mama has heard of what happened. She is calling a family meeting. So we will be Antipolo-ing this Friday at 7pm sharp. ALL IS REQUIRED TO ATTEND. Should we ride together?

Philip: Ate, it's 'ALL ARE REQUIRED.'

Chari: #grammarnazi Philip.

Merry: What is that Charity? Why did you spell it in one word? Is this that hash tag that you were trying to explain to me the other day? I think my high school classmate does this as well. What is the significance of putting a # key in your messages? I saw the baby of your niece the other day, she was very cute!

Flora: Fwd: Fauna Aguas mentioned you in a comment.

Maggie: Tita, I think you accidentally copied the wrong link.

Maggie Aguas sent a sticker to the group.

Flora: Oh Magggie, how did you do that? Show me how!

Maggie Aguas sent a sticker to the group.

Philip: Martha and I have meetings until six pm, but we will head straight to Antipolo. Might be better not to have the girls in the same car for now.

Chari: *sends a thumbs up button*

Merry: Regina and I are free the whole day tomorrow. I am thinking if I should ask Enzo to join us because she might be suspicious if I do not invite him. But I think he has work until late that evening.

Fauna: Let them suspect what they want. It's for their own good anyway.

Maggie: Tita that is scary D:

Flora: If anyone can get thse two kiddos toghether it's Mama.

Philip: Here's hoping. See you all on Friday.

"You're late," Lola May's nurse informed Dad and I as we arrived at the doorstep. I had no idea why we had to rush to Antipolo for dinner, and I wasn't really in the mood to find out. But the moment the nurse led us to Lola May's library, I knew something was up. We were never led to the library.

I hadn't been in the library since about two years ago when we hosted a family reunion here, and I hid from the other relatives while looking at Lola May's photo album from her first trip to Europe. My grandfather worked for a big Asian bank, and was always going on these trips for conferences and meetings. Lola used to say being his travel companion was her full time job, and she seemed to enjoy it.

I think that was when I said it was time I did something about my dream of going to Europe, to experience the way my grandmother had, to change the way she said it changed her. So I started putting part of my salary into a small fund, which was slowly but steadily growing.

But tonight wasn't about remembering old memories. I could see from the serious looks on everyone's faces that this was an intervention. From the way Regina gasped when she saw me, I knew I was right.

"Oh my god," she said, turning to her mother with her perfectly crossed legs. "Mom, was this necessary? I want to go home."

If I was brave, I would have said, 'Don't be such a spoiled brat, Regina.'

But I was in front of the family, so I decided to be a little more decorous. I simply rolled my eyes before I sank on the couch across her and fixed her with a glare. I remembered what Enzo said, about her internalizing what was happening to Tita Flora. I wondered if it was true.

The whole family was sitting at the side of the room, with me and Regina facing each other while my Lola held court in between us with a cane in her hand as if she was going to whip us with it. I did mention my grandmother was traditional, didn't I?

"We're here to talk about what happened between the two of you," Lola said, gesturing to me and Regina with her cane. "I want everyone out."

The family didn't need to be told twice. Regina was glaring at me the way she used to when we were kids, all pouty lips and furrowed eyebrows. Lola tutted her lips and snapped the cane against the side of the couch, making us jump. Then she glared at us.

"You girls are cousins. You grew up together. Stop fighting," she said simply.

"But Lola—" Regina began.

"Stop. Fighting."

"She's not even talking!" She exclaimed, pointing at me with an accusing finger. My teacher once said that when you pointed at someone with your finger, you were pointing three fingers back at yourself. "She was the one who's in love with my fiancée. The one who lied to everyone about Max."

"Don't bring Max into this," I said between grit teeth. "And I knew Enzo long before you knew him."

"Oh and that gives you the right to lie to me?"

"NOT EVERYTHING IS ABOUT YOU!" I finally screamed, clenching my fists. "I'm so sick and tired of putting everyone's needs first. Can't you organize your own engagement party? God knows you don't do much since you moved back a month ago!"

"Hey!"

"Martha," My grandmother said in stern warning, and I deflated slightly. I was being cruel, and I was never cruel.

But looking at Regina, the personification of everything that I wasn't (thin, beautiful, happy, pursuing passion projects for Instagram) right now brought out the worst in me. Why else was I acting so erratically?

"Fine," I said stiffly.

"You were trying to offload your guilt," Regina pointed out. "That's cruel, Martha."

"Yes, and was kicking her out of your house the best thing to do?" Lola May asked, raising her eyebrow. I'd never seen Lola go into full sermon mode for any of us, but I remember from Dad's stories that she could hold court for hours on end if she wanted. "Martha kept that secret to herself for a very long time. Telling you must have been very hard on her."

Regina said nothing, lowering her gaze.

I hid a little smile of triumph.

"Don't think you're free to snicker, *hija*," My grandmother warned me. "You're not supposed to keep things inside the way you did. It makes you binge-eat, and that's not healthy at all."

I cringed. Of course she made this about my weight. Anyone could point to a flaw of mine and connect it to my weight. A headache? It must be because of your weight. A fear of heights? It's a weight thing. I was more than my size, and I knew that. Why didn't anyone else?

"Lola, this isn't about my size," I grumbled.

"No, this is about how you aren't in touch with your own feelings," Regina said. "Which is pathetic, coming from someone who acts like she's got it all together."

"I'm not acting like anything," I snapped at her. "And obviously, I don't have it all together if I'm still doing things for you."

"The two of you are acting like children," My grandmother concluded, snapping her cane against the side of her chair. She pointed it at us. "You want me to treat you like children? I'll have you sit in corners and march right to the altar to apologize to God for your behavior."

"You're not serious, Lola." Regina said.

"Are you sure you want to test me?" Lola asked, raising an eyebrow.

* * *

Which was how we ended up sitting in Lola's bedroom while the rest of our family went out to dinner. My stomach grumbled and I was hot and uncomfortable.

"You had to fight Lola on this," I said under my breath. "Now we're never going to leave. Now were going to sitting here in this heat until our sweat turns into a gross puddle on the floor."

She said nothing.

"Of course you wouldn't know about that since you're a Londoner now."

"Can you stop that?" Regina asked. "In case you hadn't noticed, I was trying to make an effort to change things between us. You have no idea what it was like for me there."

I stopped, immediately remembering what Enzo told me. Regina had been a volunteer for cancer patients at a hospital. She must have made friends who passed, seen what they had to go through to get better. I immediately regretted it.

I looked up at Regina and felt the ice in my heart melt a little.

"Enzo told me about the cancer patients," I said. "And Lola was right. I do binge-eat," I confessed with a small voice, thinking about the pangs of hunger I got when I felt horrible or sad. Was Lola right? "Sometimes it makes me feel better."

"Oh Martha," Regina said, reaching out to squeeze my hand. I worried that Regina would still be angry with me. That no matter what I said, she wouldn't listen.

"God, Regina, I'm so sorry about this whole thing with Enzo. I don't know why I said that," I finally broke, covering up my tears with my free hand. "It's not even true anymore."

And it wasn't. I knew that now.

"I hear you," she told me. "Enzo and I talked about everything, and I get it, he's a charming dude. Plus, he sings, which I figured was a thing for you."

"You have no idea," I chuckled behind my sobs, and Regina smiled.

"Not to rag on my fiancée, but I don't think he made you happy the way you deserve to be," she said. "I know you. You would have made it happen if you really wanted, Martita."

Would I? I would never really know. It was too late now to think about what I could have done, or what could have happened. All I knew now was that my cousin had forgiven me, and we were going to be okay.

Enzo had been right, but only half-right. Regina needed me to help her with the party, but I needed her to keep me from bottling everything up inside. I could trust her with things, and I wouldn't have to keep word-vomiting all over the place.

Maybe there was still a way to make up for all that time we had lost.

"I'm sorry I tried to bail on the party," I said to her. "And the Maid of Honor thing."

"Oh honey," she said. "You can never bail on being my Maid of Honor."

"So I still have to wear that dress?"

"You know it."

* * *

We were back in Lola's house a week later, and Regina and I had been talking nonstop since that night. She and I went back to the preparations for her engagement party like nothing happened. Funny how families can forgive each other so quickly.

We became thick as thieves, making up for time we had lost. I talked to her about Tita Flora, and we both agreed that we had to be more pro-active with our support of her, which was why we had been accompanying her to the handsome oncologist she really liked to know her options.

"I didn't know this about you," Regina said, reaching over to squeeze my hand. "You never really say anything, do you, Martha? I always thought you were this master of confidence, doing things so well without trying so hard. It made me just a bit jealous of you."

"I'm not, really," I said to her. "I try very hard. I want to seem like I have everything together, or else I open myself up to worse things."

Then, over cups of evening coffee, Tita Merry called us to the den to play mahjong, and soon we were pretty deep into our second round. Lola May looked seriously over the table, her light grey brows furrowed and her fingers fumbling under the smooth back of the mahjong tile.

The tile snapped on the table, and she smiled before she placed it in the discarded tiles in the middle, the face side of the tile showing up.

"Six balls," she declared with a hint of glee.

Across her, I could see Tita Merry biting her lip. It was the only time I'd ever seen Tita Merry look nervous, cautiously picking up the tile Lola May had discarded and placing it face down with two more of the six ball tiles in her line-up.

"*Pong*," she said breezily before placing a two stick tile in the discard pile.

"Lola, did you really call us here to play *mahjong*?" I sighed, pulling a tile from the pick-up stack and letting it clack against my other tiles.

I've been playing *mahjong* since I was sixteen, since it was part of the family's New Year traditions, but Lola May never let us play with her. According to her, we didn't present enough of a challenge. So when she and Tita Merry invited Regina and I to play with them, I knew there was going to be a catch.

"Of course not, *hija*," Lola laughed, picking up the tile I discarded and placing it in her deck. She skimmed her long bony fingers over the tiles in her row before discarding the tile at the end. Seven character, of no use to anyone on the table. "We're here to discuss a job."

A job? Was there a family event coming up that I was not aware of? That never happened before. I glanced over at Regina, who shrugged.

Regina pulled a flower tile, and exchanged it for a regular suit from a separate pile. She discarded the tile she got, and I snatched it before anyone else could.

"*Pong*!" I exclaimed, matching up three of the same tiles from the character suit. "What do you mean a job, Lola?"

My sweet, seventy six-year old grandmother cackled with glee at my discarded tile and seemed to have forgotten she was asked a question.

At least I knew where Maggie's competitiveness came from.

Regina turned to her mother. "Mom?"

I laid down the tiles I'd completed and discarded four balls.

"For goodness sake, Merryweather, just tell her already," Lola said.

"*MAHJONG!*" Regina suddenly exclaimed, flipping all her cards face up so we could confirm her win. Sure enough, she'd won. Lola May started swearing like I'd never heard her swear before, and I didn't know if I should laugh or be absolutely terrified of my own grandmother.

"Martha," Tita Merry said, leaning over to me as Lola May insisted on a rematch and started mixing up all the tiles while Regina laughed. "You've been doing such a wonderful job for me, on all these charity events, and now the engagement party…"

"Oh, I'm happy to do it, Tita," I said, and I knew that it was true. For all my complaining about it, I really enjoyed helping my Aunt change things for people, for theaters and all. Plus I was getting used to talking to suppliers and putting things together.

It was stressful work, but I liked being able to see the results. Getting closer to the Met's restoration, an art workshop for at risk kids, new work by amazing Filipino artists, I was a part of it all because of Tita Merry. She took my hand.

"I'm starting a foundation," she said to me. "It will be slow going at first, but I really want to push through with the Gerund Benitez Art Foundation, and I can't think of anyone better to run it than you."

I furrowed my brows slightly in confusion. This was the first I had heard of Tita Merry's plans. I didn't even know how important the arts were to Tita Merry until she talked about it for the Met screening.

But it made sense for Regina to want to pursue something related to the field if her mother loved it. Most of Tita Merry's events, I now realized, were arts-related. But a foundation was big. It meant events, fund-raising, accountability, registrations and everything. I remember having a subject on it in college.

"…Me?" I squeaked. "But, but Tita, I don't have any experience!"

Tita Merry waved her hand over her face to wave off my disbelief. "You know how to handle clients, and your father was very forthcoming about your experience setting up foundations and other corporations. Plus you're a CPA! In fact we've been discussing this for some time now."

She had a point, but…

"Tita, I've never worked in a foundation before."

"I can help there," Regina chimed in with a little smile. "I have a couple of friends in the Royal Academy of Arts Trust in London. There's a six-month position as an Events Officer that they can line up for you."

My eyes widened, and my heart was racing so fast that my pulse was struggling to keep up. Was this really happening? I knew it sounded perfect, but a little voice in the back of my mind told me it was impossible. These kinds of things didn't happen to people like me.

In fact I was pretty sure that getting the job of your dreams and the chance to live in Europe was the kind of thing that never happened to girls like me. It was an outlier in a long line of statistical probabilities.

Ah. But you're an outlier too, aren't you? My traitorous little brain told me, and I swallowed, unable to believe this. I should just say no. I mean, why would I leave?

Lola May squeezed my arm to pull me back to reality.

"Time to grow up, and grow a pair, Martha." Lola May told me, like she was reading the doubts that were crossing my face. "This is what you want, and who you want to be. You've never apologized for being you before."

I looked at Regina, who was smiling so wide I thought her face was going to split in two.

Things happened very quickly after that. After I agreed to Tita Merry's proposal, I resigned from the office. I had my Skype interview with the RA Trust and got the position. My visa was in process, as were my work permits, my tickets were booked, and Regina was coming with me! Just for a couple of weeks though, to help me settle in her apartment, which Tita Merry let me use. My family was beyond thrilled, Dad more than anyone, really.

I couldn't help but feel that something was missing, though. I knew what it was, but I didn't want to acknowledge it. It had been a month, three days, and two hours since I'd spoken to or seen Max. He'd disappeared off the face of my life, leaving a large gaping hole where he had been. Every day I woke up feeling it pulling me apart inside, and sometimes it made me cry.

I know Regina said I could make things happen if I wanted. But I wasn't sure what Max wanted, if he still wanted me. I'd tried to get in touch with him since that day I left him, but his phone number kept coming back as 'unattended or out of coverage area.'

Save for launching a bat-signal in the middle of Metro Manila, I had no idea how to get in touch with him. The people at the clinic told me he worked on house calls exclusively now, and the book stores he frequented promised he hadn't set foot there in some time. Every Sunday, I went to Mass half-expecting to see him in his usual spot, reading a book, but to no avail. Max was gone and I didn't know how to find him.

The clock chimed to signal the time.

One month, three days, and three hours since I last talked to him.

I walked into the kitchen to get myself a glass of water. The house was empty because Mom and Dad went off to Batangas for the weekend, Benjo drove Mags to a sleepover with friends, and it was the cook's day off. I was about to leave when I heard the sounds of panting and whimpering coming from the corner. I followed the sounds, supposing Bibi just needed something from his locked crate.

"Bibi?" I asked tentatively, walking towards his voice. He whimpered before he gave a tiny, desperate bark. Now I was worried.

"Bibi, what--oh my god!" I exclaimed, seeing the state of him. There was disgusting brown vomit by his mouth, and he might have been choking on it. He was lying down and shifting uncomfortably, panting as he tried to catch his breath. My heart stopped when I saw the cause. There was an open packet of dark chocolate chips on the floor near him and it was nearly empty.

My hand flew to my phone, fingers moving before I could stop to process any of this. I moved Bibi away from the vomit to feel his tiny heart pounding in his chest. He nuzzled his face into my thigh, and I could almost hear him begging me to make it stop.

For the first time in weeks, his phone was ringing. "Please, please, please pick up," I whispered, trying to make soothing noises for him.

"Martha?" His voice rose, and all I could respond with was a choked sob. Just hearing his voice made me so happy. I didn't know where to begin. "What is it?"

"It's Bibi, he...he ate chocolate, I don't…I mean, I…" I stammered, trying to keep it together as Bibi whimpered again. "Max, I need you."

"I'll be there as soon as I can," he said quickly. "Try to keep Bibi calm, and make sure he doesn't choke on his vomit. Move him if you have to, but be careful."

Max came in thirty minutes later with his bag of supplies and a cold, hard look on his face. I was too worried about Bibi to let it bother me at the time. He found us still sitting on the kitchen floor, my dog's face in my lap and my hand rubbing his stomach gently, trying to get him to drink some water. He sat next to me, assessing him, checking his heart rate and listening to the sounds he was making. Max's brows were furrowed with concentration, and in a moment of weakness, I wondered if he was focusing on not looking at me. Which was stupid.

"How much did he eat?" He asked.

"It was already half-empty so...less than a quarter of the bag," I said as Max gently took Bibi from me. Bibi, who skittered away from Max on most days, was totally pliant. I realized my hands were trembling, and my dog would not stop whimpering. It broke my heart, over and over. "It's okay Bibi, it's okay. Max is going to make you better."

It's hard to describe what I was feeling at the moment. I suppose people with pets of their own always feel this way when something's wrong. Guilt seeped in, and my helplessness was trying to defeat me. Max worked quickly, asking me questions in a brisk tone, and retrieving something from his bag.

"We need to get the theobromine out of his system," he explained, placing a couple of black pills in his hand. "Dark chocolate has the highest concentration of that, we need to induce vomiting. I need to give him activated charcoal pills to make him throw up."

"Oh my god," I said immediately, feeling my throat tighten like I was the one about to go through it.

"Hey," Max said, the first sign of friendliness he had shown me through this whole ordeal. "I'll take care of him, okay?"

"Okay," I said with a tiny voice, looking down at my dog. He must have no idea what's going on, or what was about to happen. I was suddenly seized by a horrible thought.

What if the universe was getting back at me for what I'd done to Max, Enzo, and Regina? Max told me once that owners of Arowana fish say that when the fish died, it meant that they did it for you, dying so their owners could evade death. Had the same thing happened to Bibi? Because the only thing he'd done wrong was stick by me through this whole disaster, and...

Max squeezed my hand suddenly, and the action was so automatic for us that he didn't realize he was doing it until I squeezed back, making him jerk out of the hold immediately.

"Right," he said, shaking his head. "Let's do this."

* * *

Bibi ended up having to vomit three times until he started to calm down. I felt so bad for him, and I was sure all he wanted was to go to sleep. But thank god, Max declared that he was going to be okay just as midnight hit.

Max stayed, giving me instructions as I made sure Bibi was comfortable inside his padded crate. I left plenty of water for him and cleaned up the ugly brown vomit on the floor. Max wordlessly cleaned up the vomit on the sink.

"You don't have to—" I started.

"I want to," he insisted, his face back to that old, hard line as he cleaned up the sink. We both moved slowly, and a part of me hoped he wouldn't leave. But if I didn't say anything, he would walk out that door.

"Thank you," I said in a small voice. "For answering my call. I hope you weren't busy."

Max ran his hands under the faucet, and I handed him a paper towel before he wiped them on his jeans. Force of habit.

"No, I..." he said, accepting the towel. "I was actually supposed to meet Georg—I was coming from the airport," he finally said. "I was in New York with my parents. It's not a big deal."

The words stung me, but I tried my hardest not to let it show. I was screaming internally, and it took everything I had in me not to start yelling at him and telling him how much I loved him, how sorry I was and please, please don't make me fight with you anymore.

Max surveyed the kitchen, and I knew he was slipping from my grasp before I had the chance to tell him how I felt. I stood in front of him and grabbed his arms.

"Don't go," I said, hoping he knew how much I needed him to stay.

"Please, Max, I..."

His face softened like butter on a stone grill. The next thing I knew, my hands had fallen away and Max was kissing me. The sensation was electric, a wild storm of static and sparks that reacted to the way I felt for him. I grabbed as much of him as I could, kissing him back like he was disappearing. I found myself scrabbling for balance when his hand dipped behind a massive thigh to settle on my backside. My entire body suddenly pressed closer to his when he squeezed.

I was leaning against the counter with nowhere else to go. Displaying his impressive strength again, Max helped me up on the countertop as we kissed. I wrapped my arms around him and buried my fingers in his hair, my heart pumping with a sudden rush of adrenaline. His kisses were fuel to a flame I had kept inside of me, and it was only about to get hotter.

Getting him anywhere near me was going to be a challenge with my size, I knew, but Max was determined. How I managed to keep my balance like this I had no idea.

In several, not so graceful movements, I managed to pull my underwear down enough for Max to grab it and—in his frustration, perhaps—tear it in half. My eyes widened, and my pulse quickened.

Was there another way for me to say holy shit?

He said nothing about it, his eyes hooded and darker than I had ever seen them. But I wasn't afraid.

"Max, are you—oh!" I exclaimed, because without preamble or breath, he licked a stripe between my legs. In my shock I almost snapped my thighs between his head.

"Oh my god," I managed to say, spreading my legs as wide as I could, very conscious that he could suffocate down there. He didn't seem to care about any of that though, as he pressed his tongue into the hot, wet heat he had built up. I gasped and threw my head back, nearly knocking it on a kitchen cabinet. I couldn't grab him like this, my own body was in the way, so all I could do was lift my hips slightly towards him to encourage his ministrations.

When his fingers joined in, I was very aware that the muscles in my torso were shuddering. I couldn't keep up with him, couldn't grab him without losing my precarious balance on the counter. My heels scrabbled for something to hold me up, and Max guided them to the slightly open drawers of the kitchen cabinets, raising my knees.

"Bedroom!" I managed to gasp, threading my fingers though his thick hair. "Bedroom."

"Okay," he murmured, pulling away. He wordlessly followed me upstairs, switching off the lights after me like it was his own house. My room was pitch black when we walked in, but Max switched on the harsh, white lights, making me wince.

"No more hiding," he said to me, still with those dark eyes. I swallowed thickly.

"Okay," I agreed.

Then before I could take a breath, his lips were on mine like they had never left. His hands cupped my cheeks lightly, but I could feel the tension in his hands. Like he was trying to hold on to water. I wrapped my arms around him so tightly that his front pushed up against mine, making him break the kiss for a moment.

"I missed you, Martha," he managed to say as he took a breath.

I was so scared of saying the wrong thing again, but I wanted him to stay, so I reached for the front of his jeans, as he pulled out a condom from his pocket. I would have normally teased him about that, but these weren't normal circumstances.

We were both so ready for this that by the time he entered me, I was already halfway to an orgasm. He knew my pace and I managed to keep up, scrabbling for his back, grabbing as much of him as I could. Now who was holding on to water.

Max came first, and I wanted to be with him so badly that I pushed hard against him and made him shout. My entire body shattered, and I knew that even if I managed to pick up the pieces, I was never going to be quite the same.

He collapsed against me, this time it was his turn to curl up to my body. The only sound in the room was my own panting, my heartbeat thrumming in my ears. Like I was still up there without him.

"I...love you," I wheezed to Max in the darkness, and he looked up at me with wide, scared eyes. As if he just realized what he'd done. He pulled away and I sat back up as he stared at me.

"You don't mean that," he said, wiping his swollen mouth with the back of his hand. He got up and quickly threw on his boxers, jeans and t-shirt like nothing happened. I marched up to him.

"Max, I do!" I exclaimed, grabbing his arm and holding the sheet up. "I love you! I love you, and for what feels like the first time, I know what I want for myself. I love you because you're my best friend, Max. It's killing me that I'm leaving for London, but I don't want to go without telling you."

His eyes grew wide. I'd forgotten that he didn't know about the job yet. I opened my mouth to explain. But Max was already shaking his head. Wasn't this what he wanted me to say? Why was he trying to leave?

"I was so ready to stay angry at you," he finally said, avoiding my gaze again. "I wanted to move on and be the cool guy but...this was a moment of weakness. I love being the guy you need, Martha. You have no idea how much I wish this would be enough for me."

My emotions flared up inside me and I pulled him back again to face me. I glared at him, and it shocked me how much he wanted to look away. It broke my heart a little.

"But it can't be like this," he said. "I can't take this."

He must think I was only telling him what he wanted to hear. That I had sex with him out of...pity? But what could I do to convince him that I was telling the truth? Here I was, fighting for him, and after what he'd just done, how he made me feel...what did Max really want?

My heart was twisting inside, but I didn't let it show. I watched him feel for his wallet, phone and keys, the condom already discarded in the bin while I still there still naked. He wanted out. I could see that now. There was no point in me telling him about London if it was going to be like this. He didn't want me anymore. I could...I could learn to leave him behind.

Couldn't I?

"Okay. I get it," I told him coldly. I walked towards the door to open it, making sure that the only thing Max could see of me were my back rolls. No way would I let him see how hurt I was. "I'll swing by the clinic tomorrow to pay Bibi's bills."

He said nothing, but I heard him leaving the house, taking my heart with him. But if this is what he wanted, I knew I had no other choice.

It was pissing rain when I stepped out of South Kensington Station, but it didn't dampen my mood one bit. My workmates in the Royal Academy of Arts Trust were surprised when I explained to them that I actually enjoyed rainy days.

It helped that Dorothy Perkins and Marks and Spencer coats in the UK actually carried my size, and now I had a trench coat and a pretty umbrella to wear in the rain.

On this day in particular, I was smiling. Our boss just told us that we would be involved in the Shakespeare Live! event in Startford-Upon-Avon for the Bard's 400th death anniversary, and I could not be more excited. The rain only lifted my spirits, and even the crush of the Tube crowd couldn't dampen my mood.

The job was demanding, and the learning curve was steep, but just being a part of these events made the whole thing worth it.

Another perk of the job was that it properly distracted me from everything that had happened between me and Max. He'd vanished again, posting nothing on Facebook or any other social media platform. Regina swore up and down that she hadn't seen him since that day in her house, and Maggie said she always missed him when she took Bibi to the clinic.

I hoped that he was happy, wherever he was. It was the least I could wish him after all of this.

Who was I kidding? I missed Max, and I missed being his friend. I could take not being the one for him, but I didn't think I could take him disappearing like this.

I stopped at a crossing, jerking backwards in surprise when I realized that the light was actually green. A car whizzed past where I had been standing.

I was ten feet away from Regina's flat when I saw a figure hunched underneath the patio. I froze. I'd seen homeless people in London, of course, but not in this area. They never sat underneath other people's patios before either. The figure was shivering and wet, shaking the water from his head like a dog.

My heart hammered in my chest, and I reached into my purse for the pepper spray Tita Fauna gave me as a going away present. My fingers wrapped around a blessed rosary from Tita Merry instead. I'd left the pepper spray in the flat. Shit!

"Uhm…hello?" I asked, making my approach. I gripped the base of my umbrella hard, ready to thwack this stranger if he got aggressive. "I've got pepper spray in my purse, so…"

"What?" The stranger asked, and he looked up with sleepy, jet-lagged eyes.

It was Max.

My racing heart didn't slow for one second as I looked at him. He was still the same guy I called my best friend. He was still my Max, and nothing about how I felt for him had changed at all.

"I found your note," he announced, like he hadn't flown thousands of miles, waving it in front of me like a peace offering. It had been folded and unfolded so many times that the paper was wrinkled, and it was slightly wet from the rain.

It took me a minute for me to understand what he was talking about. The note was the piece of notebook paper I'd slipped in between the pages of Stardust, the one where I told him about how happy he made me. The one I slipped in after we had sex the first time.

I closed the gap between us and sat next to him on the porch. I took the letter from his shaking fingers, protecting us both from the downpour with my umbrella.

"And I realized that I was an idiot, leaving the way I did." he said, his elbow leaning against mine as I snuggled up to him for warmth. "I wasted my time not telling you what I wanted."

I looked down at the note, reading it over a couple of times. I had known how I felt about him all along. I slipped the note into my pocket and stood up, pulling him up with me.

"It was stupid," he kept talking as I took out the keys and walked into the flat with him following me to the kitchen while I made tea. It was the best thing to drink in the rain. "I pushed you away when I should have made you stay. I know you're happier here, but I don't want to lose you when you come back."

He followed me to the linen closet where I grabbed a towel, throwing it over his shivering shoulders as he talked about that night in the kitchen. He sneezed, and I knew he was going to get a cold. I pushed him back to the kitchen and sat him down.

"I can make you happy, Martha," Max said, sneezing again as I handed him a mug of warm tea from the counter. "I'm the guy who will do everything to make you happy."

I sat next to him and took a sip from my own drink.

"I could have told you that, dummy," I said.

Then we kissed over our warm mugs of tea while the rain poured steadily outside.

* * *

"Two cheeseburger meals, large fries, large Coke zero, and a box of chicken nuggets, please!" I yelled over to the speaker box of the McDonald's drive thru. Then I looked beside me and gave the driver a little grin. "How about you, did you want anything?"

Max laughed at my little joke as he drove the car forward to the next window. It had been about a month since we came back from Europe, and one month since Max and I officially became Max and I.

Once my job at the RA ended, he and I took that trip we'd always wanted, following a route that took us from London to Edinburgh, then to Paris, Avignon, and Provence before heading to Amsterdam, then Prague before flying to Italy, where we spent a blissful week before going back to Manila.

Max had come with everything planned out and ready, telling me he was half-expecting he would do the trip solo. We ended up sharing hotel rooms he'd pre-paid for, although I don't quite believe that the champagne and chocolate covered strawberries were with the Peninsula's compliments.

He said he wanted to make it up to me, so w and I spent the first month of dating backpacking through Europe.

I honestly don't think anyone can compete with a first date walking along the Seine and eating chocolates in front of the Eiffel Tower on the Champs de Mars. Or a walk through the flower market in Amsterdam and eating stroopwafels while cruising along the canals.

One of my favorite memories will always be watching Italian-dubbed Rocky Horror Picture Show against the side of the Castel Sant'Angelo in Rome, snuggled up in a blanket with Max. He had it all planned, and I had to admit, it made one hell of an apology.

Then we came back to Manila, and I finally felt that my life had begun. I came home with my head brimming with memories and inspiration from Europe. Tita Merry and I hit the ground running with the foundation, and despite the slight weight gain thanks to British carbohydrates and fantastic Italian pasta, I'd never felt sexier in my life.

"Careful, careful!" He exclaimed as the staff of the fast food place passed through the window. I shot him a strange look as he pulled over to the curb just so we could put the food in areas we knew they wouldn't topple over.

"What are you so worried about?"

"That dress took you forever to zip on," he said, indicating the pale pink dress Regina had chosen for me to wear to the engagement party, the same dress Max took off of my body the day he told me how he felt.

At the very least, the dress had become special, a part of our history, and I guess Max recognized that. Regina had no idea what she'd set in motion when she chose this dress for me.

"Wanna see how fast you can zip it off?" I joked, wiggling my eyebrows suggestively at him. Max laughed and leaned over, kissing my lips in the parking lot of a drive-thru. We were supposed to be on our way home from the Manila Peninsula after Regina and Enzo's engagement party, but the need to eat struck me so bad that I convinced Max to pass by the drive-thru.

"God, I am a bad influence on you," he declared, taking the cheeseburger and unwrapping it quickly to take a bite. I gave him a little french fry-filled grin.

There was a little moment of silence, then I started giggling.

"What?" Max asked me.

"Sorry. I can't get the image of you and Tita Flora disco dancing out of my head."

Max and Tita Flora had, in Maggie's words, 'burned the dance floor' when Tita Flora's favorite song came on at the engagement party. Regina took over my duties arranging her engagement party when I left for London, and I had to say, she did a great job. The room looked amazing, and there wasn't a dry eye in the room when Enzo asked Tita Merry's permission for Regina's hand in marriage.

If that wasn't enough, Regina used the money she got from Tita Flora's inheritance to start Paint Pilipinas, an organization that went around public schools in the city to give the kids a chance to indulge their creative side and paint. Some of the kids were being sponsored to learn more about art and painting, which in turn, made them more interested in the blossoming art scene in the Philippines. It was one of the Gerund Benitez Foundation's first projects, and I was thrilled to be working on it with Regina.

While I was in London, she and I constantly talked to each other, utilizing any medium possible for us to tell each other about what was going on with us. I didn't hear a lot about Enzo, but as long as he and Regina were happy together, I was too. Our days in theatre together felt like a distant memory. One that I could dig up, smile fondly at, and put back away.

"Well, you're already twenty-seven hija, your biological clock is ticking," Max teased, imitating Tita Fauna's flat, matter-of-fact voice.

After I came home from London, I realized that there wasn't a lot of difference between Max and I as best friends, and Max and I as…not best friends. We still liked the same movies, judged the same people and ate off of each other's plates.

In a way, I liked to joke, we were never really friends when we saw each other. I guess it's because we'd known that we were supposed to be like this for a long time. We knew what we wanted before either of us could recognize it.

We'd wasted a lot of time not being honest with ourselves, and I felt like we were making up for every lost second. But I was happy, happier than I ever thought I could be. Yeah I gained ten pounds living in London. So what? It didn't matter because the people who loved me, the people who mattered, thought I was perfect just the way I was. That was all I could ever need.

"Speaking of which," Max cleared his throat, feeling for something in his blazer. "I owe you something. I realize it's a little late. I was supposed to give this to you midnight of your twenty seventh birthday, but…it's better this way."

I looked down and my heart stopped.

Holy shit.

I kissed him, and he tasted like grease and salt, his fries spilling on his lap.

It was perfect.

The End

Acknowledgements

Where to start?

First of all, I have to thank my friends at #romanceclass, the clingiest group I know. We're constantly surprised by happenings and feelings, and I'm so glad I have them to support me through this CRAZY writing process.

Then of course, I also have to thank Iggy, Suzette (I still have your note!), Farrah and Carmel for beta-reading this story. They were the first ones to fall for Max's charms!

As always, a BIG thank you to my fairy godmother Layla, who encouraged (nay, lovingly demanded) the steam and chose Max's favorite song.

Thank you to Atty. Kat for directing me to Doc Racky Velasquez, who helped me with the vet stuff, and to Stacy and Danah Gutierrez of Plump.ph who answered my questions on steamy scenes and body image.

Huge thanks also go to my Mom, who came up with Tita Flora's inheritance twist over lunch, and my Dad, who fact-checked my inheritance terms.

The title (and the chapter titles, if you're reading the print edition) are by my amazing sister, Gabbie!

Sige na nga, J. Thanks na din sa 'yo.

Oh, in case you were wondering, Ava and Scott have their own story, which will soon be out in print! Look out for Midnights in Bali at a bookstore near you.

About The Author

If you ask Carla de Guzman what she does for a living, she will tell you that she's not quite sure.

By day, she works a regular day job and writes for a lifestyle website. By night, she's an author and an artist, spending her midnights at her desk and making these silly love stories. She loves to travel, coming home to her dog Kimchi and spending her weekends having dinner with her crazy family.

She's currently on a quest to see as many Impressionist paintings as she can, and is always in search of the perfect pain au chocolat.

@somemidnights

www.carladeguzman.com

somemidnights@gmail.com

Other Books by Carla de Guzman

Cities

Marry Me, Charlotte B!

We Go Together

Midnights in Bali

Setting the Stage (soon)

SHORT STORIES

Driving Home

Up All Night

Merry Christmas, Maggie! (part of the Make My Wish Come True Anthology by #romanceclass)